Why Am I Too Young?

by Alida E. Young

Cover photo by Bichsel Morris
Photographic Illustrators

Published by Willowisp Press, Inc.
401 E. Wilson Bridge Road, Worthington, Ohio 43085

Printed in the United States of America

10 9 8 7 6 5 4

ISBN 0-87406-043-5

For Meredith and Donovan

One

HAVE you ever had a crummy day? I mean a really lousy day when you wanted to yell at someone, slam doors, or pick a fight? Well, I've had a week like that . . . no, two weeks . . . ever since school let out.

You see, we live way out here in the high desert. Desert Willow has only about twenty-five hundred people. The nearest town is five miles away and the bus doesn't run on Sundays. So I can't go to the movies, the park, or even the library. Worst of all, my best friend has spent the entire week with my most unfavorite person. I guess I'm just feeling left out.

I finished my share of the kitchen cleanup after dinner. Then I looked at the TV guide, but nothing sounded interesting. Our California Spanish-style house is nice and cool, especially with the air conditioners going.

But outside it's probably still in the nineties—too hot to do anything very strenuous. I've read all my books from the library. I've reread all my teen magazines. I've polished my toenails three times with three different shades of red. What can I do? I wondered. I felt like a cholla cactus, all prickley barbs.

I went into the living room where Dad was flaked out in his brown leather recliner that Mom says clashes with the Mediterranean furniture. He was watching TV. Mom was stretched out on the couch with a washcloth over her eyes.

"Mom? Are my pink shorts in the wash? I can't find them."

"Try looking under your bed. Callie, you're old enough to take care of your own clothes. Now, let me rest for ten minutes."

She never wants to talk right after she gets home from work because she's a checker in a supermarket. She says she gets sick of listening to the electronic voice on the new computer cash register.

So I went over to my father. "Dad? Oh, Dad?"

"Callie, honey, leave him alone," my mother said. "He worked until after midnight last night."

Dad is circulation manager for a newspaper. He's always too tired to do anything because he works such long hours.

"I just wanted to ask if we could go riding in the dune buggy." Sometimes Dad lets me drive the little red bug. I don't need a license to drive on the private back roads.

"Why don't you go ride your bike," my mother mumbled.

Oh, sure. That was like telling me to go play in traffic, because except for the busy highway, all the roads are sand and soft dirt. "It's still too hot," I said.

"Then go call one of your friends."

I went out to the telephone in the kitchen. Earlier, I'd tried to call my best friend Lynn. But the line had been busy. We were supposed to go swimming tomorrow. I wanted to tell her I had changed my mind.

I tried her line again. She answered so fast she must have been holding the phone.

"Lynn? It's me," I said.

"I'm waiting for a call from Pam. Gotta go."

"Sure," I said, trying not to sound put out.

Pam Jennings lives next door to Lynn. Pam and I have never gotten along. My mother tells me to be charitable. She says Pam is going through a difficult time right now because her folks are getting a divorce. But I've known Pam for six years, and she's always been a pain. I don't know why Lynn always spends so much time with her.

I drummed on the telephone table. Who else could I call? I finally decided on Rusty. He has red hair, but he's not called Rusty because of that. His name is Russell T. Page. His mother answered.

"Mrs. Page, this is Callie. May I speak to Rusty?"

"I'm sorry. He's out riding. Do you want him to call when he gets back?"

"No," I said with a sigh. "I guess not." Anyway, all Rusty ever wanted to talk about was his horse or the plants and animals of the high desert.

I wandered into Dad's office where my ten-year-old sister Tessa was working on her computer. "What're you doing?" I asked.

"What's it look like I'm doing?" she answered, never looking away from the green letters on the screen. "That's a dumb question."

"Dumb! You're so dumb, you flunked kindergarten!"

This, of course, wasn't true. But she makes me so darned mad. Just the fact that she's a brain who has used computers since she was seven doesn't give her the right to act so superior.

"You want to play a game of Scrabble?" I

asked. I'm really desperate when I'll ask Tessa to do anything. I am good at word games though, and sometimes I can beat her.

"Nope."

"How about playing one of your computer games?" I couldn't believe I'd asked her that. I must be even more desperate than I'd thought. I was almost relieved when she said no.

"I'm too busy," she said. "I have to redo a whole diskette because somebody messed it all up."

"Don't look at me. I wouldn't touch your old diskettes."

She always blames me if something goes wrong with the computer. I have a theory that it's Barbie Doll, my cat. I named her that because on my tenth birthday I wanted a Barbie doll. But Mom thought they were sexist and that I was too old for a doll. So I got a cat instead, and I think she messes with the keys on the computer.

I wandered back out to the living room. Barbie Doll was sitting on her stool. When I tried to pick her up she spit at me, jumped out of my arms, and ran out. Boy, even my cat rejected me. I might as well go out for a walk and talk to the coyotes and road runners. They'd probably ignore me, too.

"Mom? May I go spend the summer with

Grandma?" I had to do something.

"You know she works all day. You're not old enough to be in New York alone."

"How about Granny Martha? She doesn't work." My great grandma lives in San Diego, and there are lots of neat things to do there.

"Callie, you know she lives in a retirement home, and there aren't any kids around. You were bored to death the last time you visited her."

"Then, can I have a nose job?" My nose tilts up at the end and I've never liked it. Lynn's going to be a plastic surgeon, but I don't want to wait until she's a doctor.

Mom lifted the cloth from her eyes and gave me a long look, as if wondering if I were serious. "You're not old enough to make that decision," she said.

It's really weird. When I was twelve, I was always too old to do things. "Callie, you're too old for dolls." "Callie, you're too old to be acting like a baby at the dentist." Now that I'm thirteen, I'm too young to do anything.

I noticed my dad was awake so I went over and sat on the arm of his leather chair. "Dad, would you take me to town in the morning?"

"Sorry, honey. I have to go in at the crack of dawn."

"Isn't it tomorrow that you go swimming in

the new pool in Rancho Palms?" Mom asked.

"I don't want to go. The chlorine turns my dumb hair green."

"So you'll look just like one of those rock singers you admire so much," Dad said.

"Your hair is beautiful," Mom said.

"Oh, sure, if you like thistle-blonde hair that won't curl."

"So wear a bathing cap," Dad said.

"Oh, Dad, nobody wears caps. Besides," I said, "I'll get sunburned."

"So, why did you let me buy you that new bathing suit?" Mom asked.

"I don't know!" I yelled.

"Well, you're in a lovely mood. Maybe you'd just better go to bed."

I wanted to flounce out. I've been practicing my flounce since I was a little kid, and I've got it down pat. But for some reason I burst into tears and ran to my room.

I flung myself on my twin bed, almost landing on Barbie Doll. I don't know how long I lay there, wishing I were grown up. I could go to New York and be a dancer . . . if I could dance. Or I could go to Hollywood and be an actress. That's a laugh. I even hate to get up in front of the class to give a book report. If I were an adult I'll bet I wouldn't have all these problems.

I heard the telephone ring and sat up. It was probably for Dad. There is always some disaster at work. Or maybe it was one of Mom's friends. Or it could be a computer junkie calling Tessa.

"Callie?" Mom called. "It's Lynn. You can use the phone in my room."

Not wanting to seem too eager, I ambled slowly across the hall and made myself comfortable on my parents' waterbed.

"I've got it," I called to Mom and heard the line click. "Hello," I said casually. "Is there something I can do for you, Lynn?"

"Hey, I'm sorry I had to cut you off short a while ago."

"Oh, that's okay," I said, trying to sound off-hand. I never can stay mad at her.

"Good. Pam's been helping me make a cover-up to match my suit. Wait'll you see it. It's just darling. Pam says it makes me look at least sixteen. I sure hope we don't have to wear bathing caps. It'll ruin the whole effect."

"I don't know if we do. But I haven't decided whether I'll go or not."

"What do you mean? You have to go! I'm sure not going unless you do."

"Well, I don't know . . ."

"Anyhow, it's a way to keep cool. It's supposed to be 103° tomorrow. And besides, don't you want to show off your new pink suit?"

She really sounded as if she wanted me to go. It would be cooler. And I was looking forward to wearing my new suit.

"Come on, Callie. I'll bet we meet some really cute guys."

"Cute guys?"

"Sure. Maybe we'll meet some guys from Rancho Palms. Come on. It'll be fun."

It did sound like fun. Excited now, I jumped off the bed. "Okay. I'll meet you at nine-thirty at the bus stop. Bye." I could hardly wait to try on my suit again. Lynn was right. Tomorrow was going to be a great day.

Two

THE next morning I hurried to the bus stop. Lynn wasn't there yet, but Rusty and Pam were. "Hi, everybody," I said. "Where are you two headed?"

"Swimming," Pam said and looked around. "I wish Lynn would hurry. She's going to miss the bus."

"You lucky guys," Rusty said. "I have to work today. I have a part-time job grooming horses."

Rusty has a million schemes to earn money. He takes tourists on tours to see the desert herbs and sells them. But some day he wants to be a wildlife photographer.

"It's too hot to have to work," I said to Rusty.

Even this early in the morning, the sun was hot on my face. I clapped my hand on my bare head and groaned. "At least a dozen times

Mom told me not to forget my hat."

"Here," Rusty said, holding out his Dodger baseball cap, "a few more freckles won't hurt me."

"No thanks." I wasn't about to wear his cap. Mine was a really cute white canvas one. I bought it at the country club pro shop where Lynn's mother works. Lynn's lucky because she gets all these neat sweaters and sports clothes at a discount.

I was about to give up on Lynn, but she made it just as the bus pulled up in a swirl of dust and fumes. We hurried aboard and found seats near the back. I managed to sit next to Lynn.

Pam was sitting right across the aisle. She leaned over and whispered loudly, "Kathy Page went to the opening of the pool last week. She says some real hunks showed up. I wish there were some interesting guys in Desert Willow."

Rusty, who was sitting in front of us, turned around and grinned. "Do you girls ever talk about anything besides clothes, soap operas, rock stars, and 'hunks'?"

Pam made a face at him.

The road to Rancho Palms drops nearly 1,200 feet in three miles. It loops and twists through a canyon right down to the desert floor. The yuccas, Joshua trees, and green creosote give way to clumps of tumbleweed and sand. The curves and the smell from a diesel truck in front of us were making me nauseated. "Oh, I wish I hadn't eaten the pancakes and bacon Mom forced on me this morning," I said to Lynn.

"Oh, for Pete's sake, Callie's going to get sick again," Pam said, as if I were deaf or in the next county. "Can't she take motion sickness pills or something?"

I leaned around Lynn and glared at Pam. "I'm not going to get sick." I wanted to add that if I did get sick I'd use her tote for a barf bag. Like I said, she's not my favorite person.

The temperature in Rancho Palms felt twenty degrees hotter than at home. Sometimes the temperature gets up to 118°. Movie and TV stars and rich people come here a lot. But they leave during the summer. Pam's always bragging about meeting movie stars. Rancho Palms is only a three hour drive from Hollywood. The town has been in dozens of cowboy movies. My dad says if you have to work in Rancho Palms, you can't afford to live there.

We got off the bus a couple of blocks from the park. We waved good-bye to Rusty and hurried to the pool so we'd be there the minute it opened. The new park was really pretty with lots of green grass, tall palm trees, and purple bougainvillaea.

In the locker room we undressed in the stalls. I dug my new pink suit out of my flight bag and put it on. I really loved the color. I thought I looked good in it.

Pam looked cute in her blue bikini, but her legs are skinny. Mom says I'm going to have good legs.

Lynn came out and strutted around to show off her new yellow suit.

"How does it look?" she asked.

"Great," I mumbled. I looked at her chest, then looked down at mine. I wanted to go hide under a blanket.

"Your suit is darling," Lynn said generously. "That color is perfect for you."

"Just don't get sunburned or you'll match the suit," Pam said.

I flung my towel over my head and shoulders, slunk out to the pool area, and sat on the steps at the shallow end.

Pam and Lynn jumped in and began paddling around. The pool was huge and fairly crowded, but I didn't see any kids I knew . . . or any hunks.

Then I saw him. He was a lifeguard,

bronzed, blond, six-foot-three at least. He moved around the edge of the pool like some great tawny cat.

I hardly noticed the splashes of the little kids playing Marco Polo. I didn't even notice I was still wearing my wristwatch.

Lynn, all dripping and out of breath, came over and sat on the step beside me.

"Come on, Callie, the water's great."

"Hmmm?"

"I said, come on. What are you staring at?"

"Huh? Oh, nothing."

"Your mouth is open. You're sitting there with a towel over your head. Your wristwatch is underwater. And you tell me nothing."

I nodded toward the lifeguard. He was climbing up the ladder of the chair that was high enough for him to see all over the entire pool area. "Now there is a hunk. Except in the movies, I've never seen anyone like him. He's gorgeous, wonderful. Oooh," I moaned, overacting so she'd think I was kidding. "I think I'm going to die." I leaned back and accidentally slid down into the water.

I came up choking and sputtering.

"One of these days you're going to kill yourself acting like a nut."

"Cashew!" I sneezed.

"Oh, you and your dumb puns."

I guess I do that when I don't want anyone to know how I feel.

She was staring at the lifeguard now. "He is cute, isn't he?" she whispered.

"Cute! Babies are cute. Little kittens are cute. He's . . ." I couldn't even think of a good enough word to describe him.

"What are you two whispering about?" Pam wanted to know.

I hadn't even noticed her swim up to us. I wouldn't have told her, but Lynn motioned toward the lifeguard. "Will you get a load of him? The guy wearing the T-shirt with a dolphin on it."

Pam turned to look. She squealed the way she always does.

"Ssh!" I hissed. "He'll notice us gawking at him."

"Wow. He's like those pictures of Apollo the sun god," Pam said dramatically.

Pam likes to write poetry. She gets carried away sometimes.

Lynn sighed. "How old do you think he is?"

"Eighteen, at least," Pam said positively, as if she'd seen his birth certificate.

"Come on, Lynn, let's race," Pam said.

Leave it to her to want to show off.

"You coming, Callie?" Lynn asked.

"In a minute." But I sat there watching the

lifeguard. He stood up and blew his whistle. He held his megaphone to his mouth and called, "Okay, you two boys by the diving board. No more ducking."

Even through the megaphone his voice sounded terrific. I wouldn't mind almost drowning if he were around to save me. My mind drifted.

I'm by myself on a white sandy beach in the Greek Isles. The sea is silver-green. Gentle swells roll up to my feet. Suddenly lightning zigzags across the sky. The swells become a giant tidal wave. Before I can run away the water crashes over me, sweeping me out to sea. The silver-green water rushes over my head. Fingers of seaweed swirl around me. I cannot move. I bob to the surface and cry for help. As if in answer, I see a gleaming dolphin swimming toward me. A golden-haired man is riding the dolphin. It is Apollo, the sun god. He sweeps me up onto the dolphin's back and yells, "Hi ho, Silver, away!"

I had to laugh at myself. Even in my fantasies I can't stay serious.

I pulled the towel off my head and fluffed out my hair with my fingers. Maybe I should go back to the locker room and comb it . . . maybe even put on a little lip gloss. Instead, I sat there trying to think of a way I could talk to the lifeguard without being too obvious.

I'd never felt like this before. I guess it seems silly. But I just had to talk to him, to have him look at me and speak to me personally. It was more than just wanting to get close to a famous person the way Pam does. I did think about going to him and asking for his autograph. I could pretend I thought he was some rock star. That seemed corny though.

He was climbing down the ladder now, and I was afraid he might be leaving. As I drew the towel around my shoulders, it caught on my wristwatch. Then I remembered I'd soaked my watch earlier. I held it to my ear. It wasn't ticking. Dad would give me a lecture, but right now I was glad the watch wasn't working. It gave me a perfect excuse to approach the lifeguard.

I jumped up and hurried over to catch him. "Uh, can you tell me what time it is?" I held up my arm. "My watch got wet and it's stopped and I don't know how I could have done such a stupid thing and I'm sorry to bother you . . ."

I'd have probably kept on babbling away if he hadn't grinned and pointed to a huge clock at the end of the pool area.

I felt my face flush. My stomach flipped and

took a dive down to my toenails. "Thanks," I mumbled.

As if I weren't embarrassed enough, I turned to go back to the steps and tripped over the foot of the lifeguard chair.

And who should be watching the whole darn thing? Pam. She was leaning her arms on the side of the pool. She looked up at me and gave me a wicked smirk.

She climbed out and followed me over to the steps. "What time is it, Callie? Maybe you need glasses, Callie. If you wanted an excuse to talk to him, why didn't you ask him if you could sign up for the lifesaving course?"

That wasn't such a bad idea, I thought. I put my watch in my bag, then jumped into the pool and raced to the other end and back. I'm a pretty good swimmer. I hoped the lifeguard was watching me.

* * * * *

At noon we took our lunches over to an open area away from the pool. There were benches, but most of the kids just sat on their beach towels. The cement was hot even through the heavy towel.

I dug into my sack for a peanut butter and jelly sandwich. In the hot weather no one dared bring tuna or egg salad. I'd just taken a big bite when a shadow crossed my face. I looked up.

Apollo the sun god was standing there.

"Hi," the lifeguard said. "You're the girl with the water-soaked watch, aren't you?"

The bread stuck in my throat and the peanut butter glued my tongue to the roof of my mouth. "Ughh. Yughss."

I wanted to die right there. I wanted to sink through the cement. Lynn handed me a can of warm orange drink. Finally, in a strangled voice, I managed to say yes. "Is there some rule about wearing watches?"

He grinned. "No. I just noticed you were getting sunburned." He handed me a tube. "Put a little of this zinc oxide on your nose."

He smiled down at me. I felt as if I really could melt right through the cracks of the cement. In a daze I dabbed some of the cream on my nose. "Thanks."

"Next time, use some sunscreen. You could get a serious burn with skin like yours."

With a little wave to the three of us, he went back to the pool. Lynn and Pam were about to explode with giggles.

"I don't believe it," Pam said. "I don't see why he singled you out. My skin burns just as easily as yours, but you won't catch me using that white stuff. Callie, you look like a clown."

Right now, none of her remarks could bother me.

"Did you see his smile?" Lynn asked. "I'll bet he's never had to go to a dentist in his life."

"His teeth are too perfect," Pam said. "He probably had them capped."

I forgot about eating. I hardly noticed when Lynn and Pam finished eating and went back into the pool.

Pam was right. He had actually singled me out to talk to. Me. Callie Anderson.

*　*　*　*　*

I was still in a dream at dinner that night.

"Well," Dad said, "I don't see any green hair."

"No, but she sure has a Rudolph the Reindeer nose," Tessa said.

Mom looked at me more closely. "You are a bit sunburned. Did you wear your hat?"

"I kept my towel over my head a lot of the time."

"As soon as you eat, why don't you put some lotion on your face and arms?"

"It doesn't really hurt. It's just tender."

"Just wait a little while," Dad said. "I

remember the sunburn your mother got in Crete, or was it The Isle of —"

"Yes, Dad, I know. She had blisters all over."

"It's nothing to joke about," Mom said. "Sunburns can be very serious for people with fair skin. I've told you a hundred times to be careful."

Usually I would have bristled at all their talk about my skin, but now I just smiled agreeably.

Tessa was watching me while we were clearing the table. She gave me a knowing look. "So what happened today?"

"I'm sorry, little sister, but you're too young to understand."

She stuck out her tongue and made a disgusting sound. I merely smiled at her immature display. Poor child.

Three

AS I was drying off after my shower, the phone rang. "I'll get it," I yelled, and wrapped the damp towel around me. I hurried into my parents' room and grabbed the phone. "Hello?"

"Hi, Callie, it's me."

"Hi, me, I was just about to call you. Oh, Lynny, I just can't wait to go back to the pool tomorrow."

"I can't go. I have that dumb old dentist appointment tomorrow."

"Crumb, I forgot."

"Pam's not going either. She just started her period."

I didn't care whether Pam went or not, but I hated to go without Lynn. We always did everything together. "Can't you change the appointment?"

"I've already done that twice."

I lay back against the pillows and sighed. "Have you ever seen anybody like him before?"

"Him who? My dentist?"

"You know who I'm talking about. The lifeguard."

"He's cute, all right," Lynn agreed.

"He's gorgeous. Did you see his tan? And his muscles? I mean, did you see his chest and arm muscles? I'll bet it's from swimming."

"Ummm."

"Or do you think he lifts weights?" I asked.

"Probably."

"I never thought I'd go for a blond guy. If you're blond, aren't you supposed to be attracted to dark-haired men?"

"I don't think there's any law about it."

"Did you see the way he came right over to me? How did he remember I was the one who had wrecked her watch? I must have made an impression on him."

"Well, you were sort of noticeable. Sitting there with that towel over your head, you looked like an Arab without a tent."

"I don't care. He talked to me." I looked at myself in Mom's mirrored tissue box. "You know, I hated to wash off that zinc oxide."

"So are you going back tomorrow?"

"If I can. I don't want him to forget me. I'll

tell you all about it when I get back. I promise. Lynn, did you notice his eyes?"

"I noticed his eyes. I noticed the dimple in his chin . . . and his muscles . . . and his golden tan." She giggled. "I even noticed a huge wart on his left thigh."

"You didn't!"

"Gotcha," she said, laughing.

"So, what were you doing looking at his thighs?" I asked.

"Callie?" my dad called. "Please get off the phone. I'm expecting a call from work."

"Gotta go, Lynn. Talk to you tommorow. Okay?"

"I just hope I can talk after the dentist gets through with me. Bye."

I hung up and wandered back to my room. I looked at myself in my door mirror. Not too bad, I thought. The slight sunburn gave me a nice rosy glow. I have nice eyes. Everybody always mentions my blue eyes. Dad says I have good cheek bones. I like being five-foot-six. I think it makes me look much older. But those were the only pluses I could see. I stuck out my tongue at my reflection in the mirror.

"Boy, are you weird!" Tessa said. She was standing in the doorway watching me. "Ever since you got back from the pool today, you've been acting weird."

She hopscotched her way across our room, landed in the middle of her bed, and sat cross-legged.

"Nobody invited you in here," I said. "I'm busy."

"Doing what besides sticking your tongue out at yourself?"

"I'm just trying to figure out how to improve my looks. You know, look more sophisticated."

"Wearing a towel with a picture of Bugs Bunny on it doesn't quite do it."

I ignored her and picked up my wristwatch from the dresser. I held it to my ear. It was ticking again. That had to be a good omen.

"How come you want to look sophisticated?" Tessa asked, still watching me closely.

"Just because I do, that's all. You'll understand when you're older."

She gave me that knowing smirk again. "It's a boy, isn't it?"

For the thousandth time I thought, Why wasn't I born an only child?

* * * * *

The next day I ran all the way to the bus stop. I wasn't taking any chances of missing the nine-thirty bus.

All the way to Rancho Palms I was trying to

think of excuses to talk to the lifeguard. Would he remember me? I wondered.

When I got to the park I fidgeted around waiting for the pool to open at ten o'clock. After a million years or so they opened the gate. I hurried to the locker room, changed into my suit and raced out. I didn't have my clothes with me. I ran back and jammed them into my bag and caught my T-shirt in the zipper. Finally, I tore out to the pool, skidded to a stop, and looked around for the lifeguard.

He was nowhere in sight.

In the tall lifeguard chair was a cute older girl. I felt betrayed. How dare someone else be in his place? Disappointment, heavy as a chunk of cement, settled in my stomach.

I dropped my bag and towel on a bench and dived into the deep end. I stayed under water so long I was about to explode. Maybe I'd just drown myself. But then that cute girl would try to save me, not my sun god. I came up gasping for air and found myself face to face with Rusty.

"What the heck are you doing?" he wanted to know. His face looked half mad, half concerned. "Are you trying to break a record for staying under water, or committing suicide?"

"Neither," I said, treading water, trying to

get my breath back. "How did you get here?"

"I rode Samantha."

That's his chestnut mare. There is a horse trail from Desert Willow to here, but in the summer it's usually too hot to ride a horse or a bike. "Where did you park her?"

Rusty shook his head with disgust. "You don't 'park' a horse, noodle-brain."

Horses! I think he prefers them to people. I never see him flirting with girls. He's so serious. He seems older than thirteen sometimes. Maybe it's because his father died when he was ten. I like him a lot, though. I just wish he were taller. Once in dance class, he put his head on my shoulder. I wanted to die of embarrassment. His dad was tall, so maybe Rusty will grow some more.

He turned over on his back and floated while I kept treading water. I envied him. I have never been able to float. When I was a little kid I had a theory about it. My great grandmother had gallstones. I thought I had inherited the same condition. I figured my gall was all filled with rocks and that was why I sank.

I was getting tired of treading water. "I'm going to get out for a while."

"I haven't seen Pam or Lynn," Rusty said. "Did you come alone?"

"Uh huh. Lynn's at the dentist, and Pam—she's not feeling very well today."

"Want to ride home with me?"

I looked over at the lifeguard chair. The girl was still there. "I guess so."

He flipped over to look at me. "You sure sound enthusiastic."

"My mind was on something else. Yes, I want a ride."

"I have to be home by two-thirty. Is that okay?"

"Fine." I like to swim, but since the lifeguard wasn't there, the day was spoiled for me.

I climbed out and lay in the sun for a few minutes. I glumly watched the other kids horsing around in the water. I wished I had brought a book. When my skin started to tingle I jumped back into the water. Rusty and I swam laps, raced a couple of times, and tried to see who could swim under water longer.

At noon we took our lunches over to the eating area. This time I'd had sense enough to bring cheese sandwiches, not peanut butter. Rusty began telling me about a new money-making scheme.

"I'm going to board horses while people go on vacations."

"Won't that really tie you down? You won't

be able to go anywhere."

"Sure I will. I have to feed and exercise them, not babysit—"

"Hey, Russ, how are you doing, good buddy?"

We both looked up, and I choked on my apple. The lifeguard, my sun god, was standing there. I began to cough.

Rusty slapped me on the back. The lifeguard was going to think I was a real jerk. Every time I saw him I choked on something.

He nodded to me and grinned. "Hi, again. You'd better watch out. That apple might be poisoned, and like Sleeping Beauty, you'll sleep until your Prince Charming awakens you with a kiss." He winked at Rusty.

Rusty's face turned red.

My face did its usual color act. I didn't know how to answer. I sure didn't want the lifeguard to think Rusty and I were dating or anything.

"Hi, Kurt," Rusty said. "I didn't know you were a lifeguard here." Rusty turned to me. "Callie, this is Kurt Saunders. Kurt, meet Callie Anderson."

"Hello, Callie Anderson. I'm glad to see you didn't get badly burned yesterday."

Well, not on the outside, anyhow, I thought. Inside I felt as if I had a fever. My mind and my tongue didn't seem to be working together.

"I was afraid you had overdone it yesterday," he said.

My tongue decided to cooperate. "Overdone is right. Last night I thought I'd be blistered."

"Do you live in Desert Willow, too?" Kurt asked me.

I nodded. "Rusty and I are neighbors."

Kurt sat on his haunches and gave Rusty a little punch on the arm. "Rusty's the one who told me about Muhammed."

"That's his white Arabian," Rusty said to me. "Are you going to ride him in the Pioneer Day parade this year, Kurt?"

"You bet."

"You should see his saddle and bridle," Rusty said. "He's got enough silver and turquoise to buy out a king. He needs an armored truck to follow him on the parade route."

Kurt laughed. "Are you riding Samantha or Tornado?"

"I don't know if I'll enter. I may have to work."

I tried to look at Kurt without staring. The sun shone on his skin, outlining the golden hairs on his arms and chest. A few drops of moisture glistened on his forehead and upper lip. His full, beautifully shaped lips pursed as if in a kiss.

"Callie, do you keep horses?"

"Hmmm?"

"I said, do you have horses?"

"Oh . . . no."

"It's a great way to see the countryside."

"I do that in our dune buggy. I go tootling all around the back roads."

"Sounds like fun. Well, I have to get to work. When you kids finish eating come on over to the lifeguard stand. Russ, I need to ask you some questions about Muhammed."

I stared at Rusty. Kurt wanted help from Rusty? "How long have you known him?" I asked as soon as Kurt was out of hearing range.

"We met at an auction a few years ago. Remember when I found the horse that was being neglected by some people who only came out to their cabin on weekends?"

"Yes," I answered. I didn't really remember. Rusty was always saving some animal or other.

"I got Kurt to buy the horse. Then I helped him get the poor thing healthy again."

"He must be rich to have all that silver and turquoise you talked about."

"I guess. I sure envy him his stables and corrals."

"Where does he live?"

"His ranch is not far from here—just on the

edge of Rancho Palms."

"Does he—"

"Hey, look, I'm hungry. Knock off with the questions, and let's eat."

"Okay, okay, I just find him interesting, that's all."

Rusty gave me a long look. I busily unwrapped my sandwich. We finished eating in silence. My mind was spinning with questions about Kurt. Does he live in a mansion? I wondered. I'll bet they have a butler and maids and their own tennis courts. I'll bet they have a private lake with a sail boat. Kurt would take me out sailing on a moonlit night. I leaned back on my arms and closed my eyes. Kurt had called me Sleeping Beauty. Did he really think I was beautiful?

"Want to come with me?"

"Anywhere," I said softly.

"Are you sick or something?"

Realizing it was Rusty, not Kurt, I sat up straight. "No, I'm not sick. I was just daydreaming."

"So, do you want to come with me to find out what Kurt wants?"

"Oh, I might as well," I said casually.

I followed him over to where Kurt and the cute girl lifeguard were standing. Kurt looked up and saw us coming. "Kim," he said with a smile, "this is the kid I've been telling you about who knows everything there is to know about horses."

Kurt introduced us. The girl's name was Kim—Kimberley Albright. She was cute, with sparkley brown eyes and short dark hair. She was wearing a whistle around her neck. She kept twisting the cord and looking up at Kurt in a really disgusting way. I hoped she'd swallow her whistle.

"I'm happy to meet you both," Kim said to Rusty and me. "Sorry to run off, but I have to teach a jazzercise class over in the rec room. See you in an hour, Kurt."

Frankly, I wasn't the least bit sorry to see her leave.

With his eyes on the kids in the pool, Kurt asked Rusty if he knew anybody who could break and train a wild mustang. "I had my name in for one ages ago," he said. "I finally got one. But every time I get near her she goes crazy."

I could understand that. Kurt probably affected all females that way.

"There's a guy who lives near me," Rusty said. "He used to be a real cowboy. Tabor can handle any horse. I'll ask him to call you."

I wished they would stop talking about horses.

"Thanks. I'd sure appreciate it," Kurt said.

I could see that I was going to have to learn more about horses.

"Excuse me." Kurt blew his whistle. "Okay, you two, no more rough stuff, or you'll have to leave," he called to a couple of teenagers.

"I'm going in the water," Rusty said. "It's getting too hot." He jumped in, splashing me.

"Kids!" I said for Kurt's benefit. "You must get tired of the way they act up."

"Most of them are pretty good."

"Kurt, how do you get so tan without burning?" I asked. "You're blond and fair-skinned, too."

"I have to take the sun in short doses, and I use a good waterproof sunscreen. I'm lucky because it's sunny here most of time. I never really lose my tan."

"I'll get some sunscreen. Thanks."

Of course my mother tells me the same thing all the time, but it seemed more important coming from him.

A little kid came over to get Kurt to blow up his waterwings, so I dived into the pool.

Rusty and I swam for a while and played a couple of games. Then he said he had to get home. When we were leaving, Kurt gave me one of his special smiles.

"I'm glad I met you, Callie. Hope you'll come back again."

Was he kidding? I would set up camp and move here, just to get a chance to talk to him.

I could hardly wait to tell Lynn about my day. She would never believe I had met Kurt . . . that I had actually talked to him without mumbling and stuttering around like a jerk. I had to admit though, if it hadn't been for Rusty I might never have been personally introduced to my sun god.

Four

ON the ride home up the steep, winding trail, Rusty and I were silent. The only sounds were the calls of the cactus wrens, the breeze rustling through the yuccas, and the steady clip-clop of Samantha's hooves. Quail and cottontail rabbits scurried into the brush in front of us.

Whenever we ride, I sit in front of Rusty. After the exercise at the pool, the warm day and the swaying movement lulled me to sleep.

"Wake up, Sleepy-head." Rusty whispered in my ear. "You're home."

I awakened to find his arms around me, holding me so I wouldn't fall off. "Sorry, I didn't mean to fall asleep."

"No problem. I didn't have to listen to a yacking female."

I punched him in the stomach with my elbow. "How about going around back? I don't want Tessa to know I'm home yet." I wanted to call Lynn without worrying about Tessa listening in.

Rusty steered Samantha to the back of the house.

"Thanks for the ride," I said, and slid off the horse. Rusty handed me my bag. "Are you going to the pool tomorrow?"

"No. I have to help Mom most of the day. We're making cactus jelly and candy. See you." And with a wave he was off.

I rushed into the office to call Lynn. As the phone was ringing I thought of all the things I wanted to tell her. But wouldn't you know, no one was home. She must still be at the dentist's, I thought.

I didn't want to go next door to tell Tessa I was home. I was too full of my own thoughts. I decided to go to my special place. I go there when I want to be alone and think or when I'm feeling low. I grabbed a granola bar and an orange and headed up the hill to a little clearing almost hidden by crags and boulders. Long ago somebody had planned to build a cabin. They had planted a willow tree and oleanders. And they built a rock wall to keep the dirt from eroding during the heavy rains . . . gully-washers, we call them.

I sat under the willow on an old railroad tie

and looked out over the valley. I could see our house and Lynn's in the distance.

I opened the granola bar wrapper and noticed it was a peanut butter bar. For the rest of my life I'd probably feel like a jerk again whenever I ate peanut butter. Kurt must have thought I was an idiot when I was trying to talk with my teeth and tongue twingled with gooey peanut butter. Maybe I could write a book titled, *How To Impress the Man of Your Dreams.*

Oh, if I were only good at writing poems. I'd compose one titled "Ode to Apollo." My sun god, my Apollo, carry me off . . . what rhymed with off? Carry me away. Away was easier to make rhyme. Day. May. Hay. Bay.

In one of Mom and Dad's slides of the Greek Islands there's a picture of a bay. Overlooking the water are white cliffs and an ancient ruin of a temple of Apollo. I leaned back against the tree and closed by eyes . . . .

I am sitting under a willow. A shadow falls across my face and I look up. It is Apollo. He sweeps me up onto his white stallion and we fly past the moon . . . past the sun to a magical island of white cliffs.

He lifts me off the white horse and we enter the arched opening of a cave in the side of the cliffs. The cave glows with a pinkish light.

Apollo bows and takes my arm. He leads me down, down, down a stone passageway. I see a faint blue light ahead. The sound of the surf is even louder than the beat of my heart. Apollo takes me to a table set for two.

We take our seats and he snaps his fingers. Servants appear carrying silver trays filled with huge covered platters.

"Please try the drink," he says and lifts his glass.

I look at the purple liquid. "I'm sorry, but I'm not allowed to drink wine."

"It is not wine. It is the nectar of the gods."

I take a sip. It is sweet yet refreshing, like nothing I have ever tasted before.

He motions to the platters. "Help yourself," he says. "I know they are your favorites."

A servant lifts off the lid. Mounds of peanut butter and jelly sandwiches fill the tray.

"Try the kumquat jam on extra crunchy," he says.

Before I can take a bite, a white mist rises from the sea. I can no longer see the table, nor Apollo. I am alone with only the cries of seagulls. Hot wind blows across my face and ruffles my hair . . .

I sat up with a jolt. For a moment my dream and reality were jumbled in my mind. Then I realized that the afternoon desert wind was blowing. The sun was far to the west. And wishing I could fly on the white stallion, I ran all the way to Lynn's house.

* * * * *

I rang the chimes. Lynn answered the door.

"Hi, come on in, but don't you dare laugh at the way I sound. I just got back from the dentist."

"You sound okay to me."

"Well, my lower lip feels like it's hanging down to my knees. Come on upstairs."

"You won't believe what happened to me today," I said. "You're just going to die."

"Wait until we get upstairs. It's Mom's day off and she's in the family room watching TV."

The Adams' place is lots larger than ours. They could have ten kids and still have a bed for everybody. Their house is really nice. They have white furniture and a turquoise carpet that's softer than my bed. But Dad hates the place. He says he feels like he ought to get fumigated, sanitized, and wrapped in a plastic dry cleaner's bag before he steps into their living room.

We went into Lynn's room. She has her own TV, her own phone, and one of those beds with a canopy and matching frilly white curtains

44

and spread. Mom says it's not practical in this dusty country.

We took off our shoes and flaked out on the bed.

"Boy, I'm going to brush my teeth ten times a day from now on," Lynn said. "I don't want to go back to that dentist again. But at least I don't have to have braces."

"That's good," I said, "but let me tell you about—"

The doorbell rang and Lynn ran down to answer it. I could hear Lynn say, "Oh, hi, Pam. Come on up."

I groaned. I didn't want to talk about Kurt in front of Pam.

She came in and flopped on the foot of the bed. "Hi, Callie. Oh, Lynn, guess who I saw at the Palms Mall?"

"Santa Claus," I mumbled.

"Cute, Callie. Really original. It was Joey, off the soap opera, *Young Love.* I got his autograph. Oh, he's even cuter than on TV."

She held out the slip of paper. "Look, he signed it, *To Pam with all my love because Young Love is so wonderful.*"

Big deal. The note sounded pretty dumb to me.

"That's great," Lynn said. "So what did you buy at the mall?"

"Not much. Some cooler pajamas, a pair of designer sunglasses, and a couple of new bras. Can you believe it, I've grown a whole size larger?"

Pam looked at me. "Sometimes I envy you that boyish look."

"My mother says women with Scandinavian blood mature later and keep their figures longer."

Pam ignored my remark. Her mother is already fat. "Lynn, did you show Callie the new cover-up we made?"

"Not yet." Lynn went over to the closet, which is larger than my bathroom, and took a short robe off the hanger. "Isn't it darling? I can't wait to wear it to the pool."

"You guys should have been there today, I actually met—"

"Well, Callie, do you like it or not?" Lynn broke in.

"Oh, it's really cute. I love the holey material."

"It's called eyelet," Pam said. "I think it looks as good as any designer cover-up."

I looked at the hem and buttonholes. "You two really did a professional job," I said generously.

"Pam did all the sewing."

"You ought to go into business," I said. "Bet

46

you could sell stuff to the boutiques in Rancho Palms."

"I'm not about to sit over a sewing machine every day. I plan to take voice lessons and be a soap opera star."

Last week she was going to be a fashion model. No matter that she will probably never be taller than five feet two like her mother, I thought.

I got on my knees. "Listen, you guys, let me tell you about my day at the pool. Remember that gorgeous blond lifeguard we saw yesterday? Well, I met him today. His name is Kurt Saunders, he's going to Harvard in the fall, he's rich, he knows Rusty, and he has a white stallion that he's going to ride in the Pioneer Day parade," I said almost in one breath before either of them could interrupt me.

"Oh, I know all about him," Pam said. "He's bad news. Today I asked Sandy Hill about him, and she gave me all the lowdown."

I didn't want to listen. If Lynn or I think somebody is nice, Pam will always say something bad about them. She can spoil anything with a few words. Now she was at it again. "He's rich all right," she said. "Debby Mitchell told Sandy that he was in a car accident. Everybody says he was speeding, but his dad got him off because he's a big shot in Rancho Palms."

"I don't believe it," I said. "He's just about the nicest person I've ever met."

"Anyway, what's so awful about his dad getting him off the hook for speeding?" Lynn asked.

"Because, according to Debby, who swears it must be true, he was seen out at Tony's Retreat at the edge of town. You've heard about that roadhouse, haven't you?"

We all had. People say gangsters own it.

I didn't know if the story was true, and I didn't really care. But Pam had managed to leave me with a bad feeling about him. Maybe he wasn't the perfect sun god of my dreams.

Five

THE next day I didn't have to babysit Tessa until after lunch. So I decided to go up to Rusty's for a while. I dressed in shorts and T-shirt. I even remembered to put on some sunscreen of Mom's. When I came downstairs, Tessa was watching cartoons.

"I'm going up to Rusty's, so you'll have to go next door and stay with Mrs. Bailey. I'll try to get back in a couple of hours."

"I don't need a babysitter. I'm old enough to stay here by myself."

I'd felt the same way at her age. "I don't make the rules, you know. Be sure and take your key. And you haven't made your bed."

She glared at me. "And you're not my mother, either."

"I wouldn't have you—" I stopped. I was going to say I wouldn't have her for my kid, but that seemed kind of childish.

"It will only be a couple of more years, dear." It really makes her sore when I put on my superior act. It used to bug me when people would bend down and say, all slickery-sweet, And what do you want to be when you grow up? In the same overly sweet voice I added, "Then if you've proven that you have good judgement, I'm sure Mother and Father will let you stay alone."

She stared at me with her mouth open.

"You look like a guppy in a fish tank," I said.

"And you look like a . . ."

The slam of the door as I left cut off her nasty remark. Why couldn't I have had an older sister instead of Tessa? Then I'd have someone who could give me advice . . . someone whose makeup and clothes I could borrow . . . someone who . . . would treat me like a little kid. Maybe an older sister wasn't such a great idea after all.

Rusty lives about a mile from me. He and his mom have about twenty acres of land. The house and corral are nestled against the hills with the higher mountains in the background. His grandfather homesteaded the land. Now that Rusty's dad is dead, he and his mom do all of the work.

There are lots of deserted homestead cabins

in the area. It's really sad to peek through the windows of one where nobody has lived for years and see dishes on the table, the tea kettle on the stove, and wood stacked by the fireplace. It's as if the people had intended to come right back. It sounds corny, but it makes you appreciate your own family.

As I came up the hill I saw Rusty in the corral.

He saw me and called, "Come on over."

I hated the smell of the place. "I'll wait for you here. Can we talk?"

"Sure, but I have to clean the corral."

Breathing through my mouth, I went over. He was using a long-handled pitchfork to toss horse manure into bags. He sells the stuff. People use it for fertilizer.

"I'm almost finished. I just have to feed and water the horses."

"Oh, come on. Can't you do that later? You're always feeding or watering or cleaning up after those darned horses."

He tossed one last forkful of manure into the bag, then tied it. "When you have the fun of owning animals, you have to expect the not-so-fun part."

I didn't think he ever did anything just for fun.

When he finally finished, he washed at an

outside faucet. Then he waved his hands in the air to dry them.

"Do you have time to walk, or do you have to make that cactus jelly now?"

"Mom and I finished the jelly early this morning." He looked at his watch. "Sure, I have some time."

We headed up the trail to a box canyon where we like to look for Indian relics.

"What's up?" he asked.

"Oh, nothing much. I just heard something about your friend Kurt Saunders and wanted to find out if it's true."

"He's a nice guy, isn't he?"

"Well, Pam heard differently." I repeated what Pam had said about the accident and Kurt's drinking.

"I know he had an accident and that he wasn't cited for it. But I've never seen him take a drink, not even beer. He's too much into physical fitness to drink or smoke or take drugs. Pam's just passing on gossip."

I gave a little sigh of relief. "I didn't really believe her, but I'm glad he isn't that kind of person."

Rusty stopped walking and looked at me. "Why?" he asked.

"What do you mean, why?"

"You just met him. Why should you care?"

"No reason," I answered. " I just thought he was nice. And . . ."

"And you go for him. He affects all women that way. I've noticed how they look at him. They practically drool when he talks to them."

"Don't be silly. I certainly didn't drool. I thought he was very interesting."

Rusty shook his head. "All we talked about were horses, and you're about as interested in horses as I am in needlepoint."

"I am too interested in horses. You know I enjoy riding with you. But you never have the time to teach me anything about them. Maybe I could help you get Tornado ready for the parade."

We walked in silence for a while.

"Callie, did you mean it? I mean, would you really like to help me get Tornado ready for the parade?"

"Sure. It would be fun." As long as I didn't have to shovel manure, I thought.

"Let's go back. I need to put her through her paces, but I never have time. I could show you, and maybe you could work with her sometimes."

"Sure, I guess I could do that."

We headed back to the corral. I had watched lots of parades but I didn't know there were so many things you had to do.

We had to teach Tornado to hold her head high. Then Rusty buckled weights onto her front legs just above the hoof. That was supposed to make her step higher.

"I'm going to enter Tornado in the Working Western category," Rusty said. "Tabor used to be a real cowboy, and he's going to loan me some fence pliers, a lariat, and hobbles to hang from the horse."

I didn't say anything, but I was more impressed with all the silver and turquoise that Kurt was going to have on his horse.

I think we must have taken the brown and white pinto around the corral dozens of times.

By the time I got home, Tessa was furious because I was so late.

"Now I don't have any time to work on my computer. You're mean, Callie."

"I was helping Rusty with his horse."

"Oh, yeah!"

Oh, yeah is her usual come-back.

She headed straight for the office with me following her. I wanted to check the answering machine to see if Lynn had called. The only call was from Dad saying he would be home for lunch.

Tessa had already powered up the computer. She was hitting the keys furiously as if she were writing the most important thing in the world. I crossed to the desk and looked over her shoulder.

"What are you working on?" I asked.

"It's private!" she cried, and put her arms over the screen. "Don't you dare read it."

"What makes you think I'd want to read some stupid thing you wrote?"

"Well, just don't, or I'll tell Mom you're in love with a lifeguard."

"You do, and I'll erase everything on your diskette!"

"You'll do what, young lady?"

I swung around to find Dad standing in the doorway.

"She's going to erase everything!" Tessa wailed.

"I was not. I just said that because . . . because . . . she's a pest."

"Oh, yeah! It's because I overheard her and Lynn on the phone the other day."

I turned and gave her a look that said, if you say one more word, I'll get you for this.

"Well, I don't want any more of this arguing," Dad said. "Callie, that computer is for all of us to use, but the diskettes are as personal as someone's mail. I don't ever want to hear you say you'll erase a file. Is that understood?"

"Yes, but why can't I have some privacy?

Why can't I have my own room? Why can't I have my own phone?"

"We've been over this too many times. There are three phones in this house. I should think you could find enough privacy on at least one of them."

"But she listens in on the extension," I said.

"I do not! But sometimes I can't help from hearing you talk to Lynn."

"That's enough. Both of you. Callie, since we don't have another bedroom, you're going to have to try and get along with your sister. Now, I don't want to listen to any more of this bickering. All right?"

"Yes, Daddy," Tessa said.

"Yes, Dad," I mumbled.

"Now, what did you fix for lunch, Callie? I'm on my way up to Yucca Trails, and I only have a half hour."

"I'm sorry, Dad. I didn't get your message until a few minutes ago."

I rushed out to the kitchen and opened a can of tomato soup. I put a cup of it into the microwave oven. "Tessa, you butter the bread while I open the tuna."

I spread on the tuna and slapped the bread together. I plopped the sandwich onto the paper plate Tessa had ready, poured ice tea into a tall glass, and called, "It's ready, Dad."

Tessa and I grinned at each other. "We're the fastest lunchslingers in the West," I whispered.

Dad sat down at the kitchen table, took a bite of the sandwich, and choked. "That's the driest sandwich I've ever tasted."

I made a face. "I think I forgot the mayonnaise." I hurried to the fridge, got the jar, and slathered mayonnaise over the tuna. "I'm sorry. I was in a hurry."

"That's all right, Callie, but you had better put more time and thought into fixing dinner tonight. You're old enough to take your responsibilities seriously."

Tessa was looking smug.

"That goes for you, too, Tessa. Your bed isn't even made yet."

I gave her an I-told-you-so look.

Dad took a drink of his soup. "Eggh." He stirred it with a spoon. "You didn't put any liquid in it. It's like eating tomato pudding."

"I'm sorry, Dad."

"That's the third I'm sorry in ten minutes. I'm sorry just doesn't cut it, Callie."

"Here, let me fix it," I said.

"Never mind, I've lost my appetite."

"I'm sor—you'll get a good dinner tonight. I promise."

After Dad left for work, I started to call

Lynn. Then I remembered that Wednesday was her gymnastics class.

While I straightened up the kitchen I watched my favorite soap operas. But today my mind was more on Kurt Saunders. I could hardly wait for tomorrow. After the workout with Rusty and Tornado, I would be able to discuss horses with Kurt.

I spent the rest of the afternoon listening to records, watching the soaps, and reading an old horse book Rusty had given me two Christmases ago. I'd never read it. I got so interested in it I forgot to keep track of the time.

It was five o'clock by my watch. I hurried to the kitchen. We have a blackboard where Mom tells Tessa and me what we're supposed to do about dinner. My list is always longer than hers. Tonight Mom was bringing home barbecued chicken from the supermarket where she works. I was supposed to make a salad and cook the vegetable.

I had cut up the zucchini and was scraping carrots for the salad when the phone rang. It was Lynn.

"Hi, Callie, have I ever got something to tell you about the lifeguard you think is so neat."

"If it's more of Pam's gossip I don't want to hear it."

"It's not gossip. And it's two things. One's good, and one's bad."

"Tell me the good first. Just a sec, Lynn." Tessa had come into the kitchen to find out who had called.

"I don't want to talk about it on the phone," I whispered. "Can you come over?"

"I have to wait for a call from Mom. I shouldn't even be on the phone now. Why don't you come over here?"

"Darn, I'm fixing dinner," I said.

"It won't take very long."

I turned to Tessa. "How about you watching the zucchini and making the salad for me? I'll owe you one."

"Okay, but it's a big, big, big one."

"I'll be right back."

On the way to Lynn's I tried to guess what she had found out about Kurt.

Six

LYNN and I went out to her patio to talk. "Okay," I said, "give me the good stuff first."

"Well, when I got through with gymnastics class I went over to the pool for a while. I heard some kids talking to the cute lifeguard about a lifesaving class. He's teaching it. Isn't that perfect? You can take the course and get *personal* attention. You know, with his arm around you. . . maybe even mouth-to-mouth resuscitation. If I weren't taking gymnastics, I'd sign up, too."

The thought of Kurt's arm around me . . . his lips on mine was even better than my fantasies.

"How long does the course take?" I asked. "How many days a week is it?"

"I don't know."

"That's okay. I can find out tomorrow."

"Now for the bad stuff."

I could feel my back stiffen. Part of me didn't want to hear this. Part of me did. "Is it really bad?"

"I think so. When I was at the pool today, a bunch of really cute high school girls came in. I think they had something to do with the Miss Rancho Palms contest. Anyway, they were pretty enough. And you should have seen their suits," Lynn went on.

"Okay, okay, but what about Kurt?"

Lynn sighed. "Maybe I shouldn't say any—"

"If you don't tell me this minute, I'm going to scream."

"He was flirting with them. Not just with one, but all five. I actually heard him repeat the exact same line to three of them. It was fun watching, kind of like our soap operas."

"So, he was flirting. Big deal. Most guys flirt."

It's my theory that when a boy flirts he isn't very serious. If he doesn't flirt with you, but pays a lot of attention to you, that's when you can tell he likes you. Not that I've had much personal experience on the subject.

"I thought you had something awful to tell me," I said. "And by the way, that stuff Pam was telling about him isn't true. Rusty knows him and says Kurt doesn't drink or smoke."

"Maybe so, but I'll bet he's a girl-chaser."

"He doesn't have to chase girls. They chase him." I looked at my watch. "Oh, no, I'm going to get killed if I don't have dinner ready when my dad gets home."

As I was leaving, I called, "You're going to the pool tomorrow, aren't you?"

"Sure. I'll meet you at the bus at nine-thirty."

I rushed home. I got there just in time to save the zucchini from burning, but not soon enough to stop Tessa from making the salad.

At dinner Mom took a bite of the salad and looked at me. "This is a very nice . . . well . . . unusual salad tonight. Where did you get the idea of adding chocolate chips to raisin and carrot salad?"

"I made it," Tessa said proudly.

Dad hid a smile. "Very creative, Tess."

Mom asked me about my day, and I said I had helped Rusty with his horse. "Lynn and I are going to the pool tomorrow."

"You can't," Tessa said.

"Why can't I?"

"Because Mrs. Bailey has to go to the doctor."

"For Pete's sake, why didn't you tell me before?" I moaned.

"I forgot," Tessa said.

"Oh, Mom, do I have to babysit her tomorrow?"

"Why don't you take Tessa with you?" Dad suggested.

"No!" Tessa and I said together.

"Why don't you want to go swimming?" Mom asked Tessa.

"I'm working on an important project on the computer."

"You need to get outdoors more. It will do you good to go to the pool."

"Mom," I said with a groan, "do I have to drag her along?"

"It won't hurt you one bit. No more argument. Just see that you're back in time to start dinner."

*   *   *   *   *

The next morning I dragged Tessa down to the bus stop. She grumbled the whole way. Any normal kid would want to go swimming, but I had to be saddled with a weird little sister.

This day wasn't starting out the way I'd hoped. First there was Tessa. Second was seeing Pam waiting with Lynn. Pam was wearing a ridiculous pair of sunglasses that looked like the blue mini-blinds in my bedroom. Tessa snickered. She doesn't like Pam much either.

We all piled onto the bus. Tessa wanted to sit in front behind the driver. I went to the back with Lynn and Pam. Only this time, Pam sat next to Lynn. I took the seat across the aisle, closed my eyes, and pretended to be asleep. It's a trick my dad uses when he doesn't want to talk to anybody. I didn't care what Lynn had said about Kurt flirting. I wanted to think about him, to picture him in my mind. Kurt Saunders . . . Kurt Saunders . . . the bus tires seemed to whisper his name.

When we arrived at the park, an ice cream wagon was in the street outside.

"Callie, can I buy a cone?" Tessa asked.

"No." I was too anxious to get inside. "Maybe when we eat lunch," I said.

I hurried to the dressing room to change. I was ready first. "I'll meet you guys by the pool," I called and rushed out into the glaring sun.

For a moment I could see nothing. Then I saw him. My sun god was talking to Kim, the cute girl lifeguard. His arm was around her. His fingers lightly touched her tan shoulder. My own shoulder tingled as if he were touching me . . . but it was probably just the hot sun.

There were some bleachers right next to the lifeguard stand. I took a seat on the bottom row, put on my sunglasses, moistened my lips, and waited for Kurt to notice me.

He was talking to Kim about politics. I wasn't sure whether to be glad or not that he belonged to the same political party as my folks.

"Callie?" It was Tessa.

"Go away," I whispered.

"I have a knot in my strap."

"I wish it were in your tongue," I muttered. I fixed her strap and tied it around her neck. "Now, go in the water," I whispered, "before I choke you with your own suit strap."

"Aren't you coming in?" she asked.

"After a while. Now, go on."

Then Pam came over and plunked down beside me. She was wearing a gallon of suntan lotion, her dumb mini-blind glasses, and a straw hat. She's always copying some famous person. She turned on her transistor.

"For Pete's sake, do you have to play that thing so loud?" I had to strain to hear Kurt and Kim.

"Hey, Callie, come on in," Lynn called. "The water's great."

I motioned toward the two lifeguards, hoping she would get the idea.

Now Kurt and Kim were into a discussion of outer space warfare, which was pretty interesting. But when they started talking about problems in Central America, they lost me. Boy, I was going to have to start reading the newspaper and watching the TV news so I could understand what he was talking about.

Just about the time I was getting so bored I could hardly sit still, Kurt began telling Kim about his family's schooner that was large enough to sail around the world. I could see myself standing on the deck with my hair blowing in the wind.

"You're going to burn to a crisp," Pam said.

"No, I won't. I have on a sunscreen that Kurt told me about."

Pam made another face, and I hoped someday it would freeze that way. "If he told you to smear yourself with chocolate syrup, you'd probably do it."

"Can I have a chocolate ice cream cone?" Tessa asked.

"No." I turned back to Pam. "You're just jealous because you have never met Kurt personally." I didn't try to hide my smug smile.

"He doesn't even know you're here."

I turned to look at him. He was smiling at Kim. Then, almost as if he felt my eyes on him, he turned and glanced over my way. I looked down and busily picked the frayed edge of my towel. When I looked up again, he was walking toward us. I swear every drop of blood in my body went racing to my face. I sat there with a dippy smile on my face and two kangaroos using my stomach as a trampoline.

He grinned at me. Well, actually he smiled at all of us. "Hi, kids."

"Hiiiii," Pam gushed.

"Hello, Callie."

He had actually remembered my name. All I could do was smile.

Pam nudged me. "Aren't you going to introduce me?"

Then Lynn came hurrying over. I introduced everyone. "Kurt's a friend of Rusty's," I said.

"We're all friends of Rusty's," Pam said quickly. "I've known him all my life."

Rusty was right about females drooling over Kurt. Even Pam seemed to have forgotten her objections.

"I need to talk to Russ," Kurt said. "Is he coming today?"

"He has a lot of work to do at home today," I said before Pam could interrupt again. "I could give him a message."

"Thanks, I'd appreciate it. Would you ask him to call me at home tonight?"

"Sure," I said.

"Have fun, kids." And he gave us all this wonderful smile of his.

"Oooh, he's wonderful," I said. Lynn gave a long, drawn-out sigh. Even Pam didn't say anything bad about him.

Tessa looked bored. "I want an ice cream cone," she said.

* * * * *

By noon the temperature had gone up to 108°. The pool was packed with kids just trying to stay cool. The four of us took our lunches under the bleachers where there was a little shade. Tessa gobbled down her sandwiches and cookies so fast, you'd think she hadn't eaten for a year. She was finished before I'd eaten half a sandwich.

"I don't feel so good, Callie."

"That's what you get for eating like a pig."

"Can we go home?"

I still hoped to have a chance to talk to Kurt. "In a little while," I told Tessa.

"I think I'll go to the Palms Mall," Pam said. "It's cool in the stores. The Music Master is having a record and tape sale. You guys want to go?"

"I do," Lynn said. "It's too hot here."

"I want to stay," I said. "I . . . uh . . . I want to give Tessa some swimming lessons."

"The pool's too crowded to swim," Lynn said.

Pam caught me looking through the bleachers at the lifeguard chair. "Callie has a crush on that lifeguard," Pam said, so loud that I was afraid Kurt would hear her.

"I do not!"

"So how come you're all goopy-eyed when you look at him?" Pam asked.

"I'm not goopy-eyed, for Pete's sake."

"Well, I don't blame you, Callie." Lynn sighed. "He's really cute."

"You two go on." I told them. "I'll call you later, Lynn."

Tessa and I stayed under the bleachers for a while, but it was getting too hot even in the shade.

"I want to go home," Tessa whined.

"You can have that ice cream cone for dessert."

"I don't want it now."

"Come on, Tess. Let's get in the pool. You have to learn to swim."

"I don't want to learn to swim. I want to go home."

"Look, I didn't want to drag you along today, so cut out the whining. If you let me teach you how to kick properly, I'll make your bed for a week."

"Deal!" Tessa said quickly.

I figured Kurt would notice us and I could impress him. But when we climbed out from under the bleachers, he was headed out with a red-haired girl. He had his arm around her waist.

Why is life so cruel? I wondered. Why wasn't I born a redhead?

I showed Tessa how to kick properly and how to breath. But it was hard to do much with so many kids in the pool. After an hour Kurt came back, this time with a blonde. That made me feel better. At least he didn't have anything against blondes.

I wished there were some way to see him when the place wasn't so crowded. Then I remembered what Lynn had said about the lifesaving course.

"I'll be back in a minute," I said to Tessa. "Practice your kicks." I hurried over to Kurt. But before I could get his attention, he had to stop some kids from running on the deck. "Kurt?"

He turned and gave me that dazzling smile. I almost forgot what I wanted to ask him. "Uh . . . I . . . uh . . . heard you teach a lifesaving class. I think I'd like to take it."

"Great! The Red Cross has a Basic Rescue course for eleven-year-olds and up. But having seen you swim, I expect you're interested in Advanced Lifesaving for fifteen-year-olds and up."

"But I'm not—I mean I guess I need to start with the Basic Rescue." I couldn't figure out why he'd think I was fifteen, but I sure wasn't going to say anything.

"You have to complete a swimming test and have your certificate for Basic Water Safety. Kim teaches that."

"I had that last year."

"Good. We meet on Mondays, Wednesdays, and Fridays for a couple of weeks, depending on how large a class we have. It's from three to five in the afternoon."

"Ooh," I groaned. "I'll get home so late."

"I don't like giving it so late, either. But I have to do it after the pool closes."

"I'll figure out some way. Will it cost anything?"

"You'll need fins, a mask, and a snorkel. But don't buy any until I tell you what kind. Kids keep showing up with cheap, unsafe equip—"

"Callie! Callie!"

It was Tessa. She was trying to climb out of the pool. "That's my sister."

Kurt ran ahead of me and lifted Tessa out

71

of the water. He looked so neat.

"I just feel sick to my stomach," Tessa said. "Callie, can we go home?"

I looked at the big clock. "The next bus won't come by for another forty minutes."

"Look, I'm off in ten minutes," Kurt said. "I'll take you two home. I want to see Rusty, anyhow."

"Oh, that's wonderful of you. We'll hurry up and get dressed."

"I'll meet you at the entrance."

Tessa couldn't have picked a better time to feel sick. As I helped her to the locker room, I gave her a hug.

"Ugh! Don't do that. I feel bad enough already."

But I had never felt happier. I was actually going to be with Kurt.

Seven

TESSA started to climb into the front seat of Kurt's silver-gray convertible. "You'd better sit in back," I told her. "You might have something catching."

Kurt laughed. "We won't worry about that. But you'll be more comfortable stretching out." He helped her into the back. "Are you okay?" he asked.

"I just feel a little ookie, is all."

"Don't you dare throw up in this car," I whispered.

I got in front and was having trouble with the seatbelt.

"Here, let me help you," Kurt said. "I keep meaning to get this thing fixed."

He reached across me to find the end of the belt. I didn't move a muscle. I didn't even breathe. He drew the belt across my chest, fastened the clasp, and started the engine before I took another breath.

He glanced at me. "I hope you aren't feeling sick, too," he said. "You look a bit flushed."

The wind lifted the hair off my neck and cooled my face. If I felt any better I'd explode into a million pieces and all the little pieces of me would float on the breeze. "I'm fine," I said.

He drove slowly around the sharp turn so Tessa wouldn't get sick.

I slid my fingers over the maroon leather seat. I had never imagined that leather could feel so soft. "This is a wonderful car. I've always liked convertibles."

"It's great except when I get caught in a sandstorm with the top down. I envy you driving the dune buggy, though. That must be lots of fun. Is it licensed for the highway?"

"Oh, sure. Dad even takes it to work sometimes."

"I'm surprised you don't drive it to the pool instead of taking the bus."

So that was why he thought I was older. He had assumed I was old enough to have a driver's license. I turned to see if Tessa was listening. Her eyes were closed.

"Dad doesn't like me to drive on the highway." Well, that was the truth.

"There isn't much protection in a dune

buggy, that's for sure," Kurt said.

"And they are even bumpier riding than a horse. Do you ride in the parade every year?" I asked.

"I have ever since I was about Rusty's age."

"I'm helping Rusty get Tornado ready. He doesn't have enough time."

"Rusty's a great kid. Since his dad died, I've tried to be a sort of big brother to him." He looked sad for a moment, then asked, "What does your dad do?"

"He's circulation manager for the Palms Daily Journal."

"Anderson. Is Jim Anderson your father?"

I nodded.

"Some small world. I had a paper route when I was a kid. Your dad taught me plenty about handling money and responsibilities."

"Oh, he's big on responsibilities."

"Tell him hi. Ask if he remembers the skinny blond kid who kept throwing the paper through screen doors."

A sun god could never be a skinny little kid carrying a paper bag. I didn't even want to think about such a thing. I quickly changed the subject. "Where do you keep your yacht? There aren't a whole lot of places to sail in the desert."

He laughed. "We have a place in San Diego.

I've been trying to get Rusty to come down and have some fun for a change."

"My great grandmother lives in San Diego. We go there a lot."

"I'm going down this weekend. If you go, call me, and I'll take you out in the Blue Dolphin."

"You mean it?"

"Sure. Your little sister would get a kick out of it, too."

Oh, her. I'd almost forgotten she was in the backseat. "I think she gets seasick," I said. I didn't really know if she did or not, but sometimes she got carsick.

"I hope she's okay. She probably had too much sun and water. When you bring her to the pool again, see that she only stays a couple of hours."

The trip to my house seemed much too short. He let Tessa out. She thanked him for the ride and hurried in to the house.

"I'll be right in," I told her.

I got out of the car slowly and kicked at the sand with the toe of my sneaker. I wished he didn't have to leave. "Thank you for bringing us home. I really appreciate it."

"My pleasure. Maybe I'll come back sometime and you can take me for a ride in the dune buggy."

I gulped. "I'd like that."

"I'll be seeing you at the pool. Hope you sign up for the course."

"Oh, I plan to."

I watched him take off in a swirl of dust. Then I raced into the house to call Lynn, but Tessa was already at the computer in the study.

"I see you're feeling better. Don't forget to hang up your wet suit."

"Yes, Mother," she said sarcastically.

"Don't get smart. I'm going upstairs to phone Lynn. And don't go listening in on the extension."

I hurried into my folks' room and flopped on the bed. I would have burst with my news if Lynn hadn't been home, but she answered the phone.

"It's me, Callie. You'll never guess how I got home today."

"You walked."

"You've got to be kidding. Guess again."

"In a taxi."

"I should have said, Guess who brought me home."

"Who? Oh, you don't mean . . . "

"Yes, Kurt. Kurt drove me home in his convertible. Can you believe it?"

"What did you do with Tessa? Drown her?"

"Oh, she was asleep in the backseat. And

Lynn, he invited me out on his yacht." The word yacht came out in a squeal. "And he wants to ride in our dune buggy. He's even nicer than I thought. He's wonderful. He's so considerate, so . . . " How do you describe a sun god? I wondered.

"I'm happy for you," Lynn said. But I didn't think she sounded very enthusiastic. "Guess what I bought today?"

"A new album."

"No. Pam helped me pick out my new practice outfit. It's really cute. Pam says I have too much bust and hips to be a gymnast."

"Oh, never mind her. She's just jealous because she's too clumsy to be a gymnast."

"I guess. Hey, want to go to the matinee tomorrow?"

"I'd like to, but I have to go to the pool. I want to sign up for the Basic Rescue class. It's on Monday, Wednesday, and Friday."

"Is it like lifesaving?"

"I guess so. But you have to be fifteen to take the Advanced Lifesaving class. This will be fun. You learn to use a snorkel and mask and stuff. You're going to take it, aren't you?"

"I have gymnastics class. Remember?"

"It won't be much fun without you there."

"I doubt if you'll notice anybody but that lifeguard."

I laughed. "You could be right."

"Listen, Callie, I promised to call Pam. Talk to you tomorrow. Okay?"

"Sure." I hung up. For some reason, I felt let down. Lynn hadn't seemed very excited about Kurt. Oh, well, she's probably just envious, I thought.

I hung my suit outside to dry and took a fast shower. Then I hurried downstairs to start dinner. I wanted to fix something special so Dad would be in a good mood when I ask if I could take the Basic Rescue course.

"Tess," I called. "You're supposed to fix the tossed salad. And no chocolate chips this time."

* * * * *

At dinner Mom asked if we'd had fun at the pool. "Now aren't you glad you went, Tess?"

"No, I got sick."

Mom looked all concerned, ready to get the thermometer.

"She's fine now," I said. Ever since Mom went back to work, I think she overdoes the mother bit. Pam says that's because she feels guilty leaving us every day.

Dad took a big helping of tossed salad, then started poking at it with his fork. "What in the world's in the salad this time?"

"I told Tessa not to put in any chocolate chips."

"It's not chocolate chips. It's . . . popcorn." He took a bite. "Actually it's not too bad. I think we have a budding chef here."

He seemed to be in a good mood. Now was the time to ask. "Mom? Dad? May I take a Red Cross course at the pool? It's called Basic Rescue. I'll learn how to save myself and Tessa, too."

"Sounds like a good idea," Dad said.

"I'll need to buy a mask and swim fins."

"Can't you kids do anything that doesn't cost money?"

"I'm more interested in how much time you have to put in," Mom said.

"Two hours on Monday, Wednesday, and Friday." In a lower voice I added, "From three to five."

"Well . . . I suppose three days won't hurt," she said.

"What about me?" Tessa asked. "I don't want to spend all day at that dumb pool."

"You can stay with Mrs. Bailey," I said.

"No, she can't," Mom said. "Mrs. Bailey's going up to Oregon to visit her grandchildren. She won't be back for two weeks."

"Can't we get another babysitter?"

"Everybody else charges an arm and a leg," Dad said. "It won't hurt Tessa to go along, and it won't hurt you to put up with her. Just don't go to the pool until afternoon."

I knew there was no point arguing. But I was going to see if I could find another babysitter who worked cheap.

After dinner I cleaned up the kitchen, then went out to the living room where Dad was watching the news. I sat on the floor beside his recliner.

"Is there anything on about the problems in Central America?" I asked.

He looked down at me with a surprised look on his face. "Since when are you interested in world events?"

"Oh, I heard someone talking about it today, and I didn't know a thing about it."

"I think there's an article in last Sunday's newspaper. And let's see, there's one in *Newsweek*."

"That's enough," I said. I wasn't that interested. "I'll read them tomorrow. I think I'll go upstairs. I'm kind of tired."

Mom had just come into the room. "Callie, I hope you're not overdoing the swimming. You'd better stay home tomorrow."

"Mom!"

"You heard your mother. You can wait until

Monday when you start the class," Dad said.

Four whole days before I'd see Kurt again. At the door I stopped. "Dad, can we go to San Diego this weekend? I haven't seen Granny Martha for over a month."

"Not this weekend, honey. I have to work Saturday. Maybe the next."

Only Kurt probably wouldn't be there next weekend. Life was just one problem after another.

Eight

THE next morning I took the Roadrunner Transit bus into town to get a bunch of library books. If I had to stay home from the pool, at least I'd be learning something useful. I didn't want Kurt to think I was stupid. I checked out books on horses, yachting, and lifesaving.

When I got home I saw Rusty's chocolate brown Lab tied to the back porch. He was barking at Barbie Doll who trotted past him with her nose in the air. She was haughtily swishing her tail.

As I came into the house and dumped the load of books on the hall table, Rusty and Tessa came out of the office.

"Hi, Russ," I said. "Why aren't you shoveling manure or house-sitting or doing yard work?"

"I started earlier than usual and got

everything done so I could ask you to go with me today."

"Go where?"

"It's a special place I found. I haven't told anyone else about it."

"Can I go, too?" Tessa asked.

He touseled her hair. "Not this time. I want to talk to Callie. Next week, I'll take you riding on my horse. Okay?"

"Promise?"

"Cross my heart."

"You can take her today," I said. "I have too much to do."

"Can't it wait?" he asked. "This is really important to me. It'll only take a couple of hours. I packed us a picnic lunch, and I brought Cocoa along to scare away any rattlesnakes."

He looked so earnest and solemn, I thought he must have a really serious problem. "Okay, if we aren't gone too long. Tessa . . . "

"Yeah, yeah, I have to go next door again. Boy, I never get to use the computer. I never get to do anything."

Rusty grinned at her. "It's tough to be a kid."

It's even tougher being thirteen, I thought.

"You'd better change into jeans and a long-sleeved shirt. It's a brushy area. And wear old tennis shoes. We'll be wading through some marshy spots."

"A marsh here in the desert?"

"I told you it's a special place. I only found it by accident when Cocoa chased after a rabbit."

I dressed in an old shirt and jeans. I remembered to wear my hat, and also the sunscreen. By the time we got started it must have been nearly 98° and it wasn't even noon yet. I'm glad I don't live in New York. When I visited my grandmother last August I couldn't believe the muggy heat. Here in the desert it's a dry heat, and you don't feel all sticky and prickley.

We headed down Big Horn Canyon. Cocoa ran ahead chasing rabbits and quail, and hopefully scaring any rattlers lurking in the rocks.

"Did you see Kurt Saunders yesterday?" I asked.

"Uh huh."

I waited for him to say why Kurt wanted to talk to him. "Well?"

"Well, what?"

"He sounded as if it were important," I said.

"He just has some work he wants me to do."

"Have you ever been to his place?"

"Sure. It's nice."

"Did he tell you I'm going to take a Red Cross class?"

"Yes. I've been telling you ever since you were eleven that you should take it. You'll need a mask and fins. You can borrow mine if you want."

"Thanks. My dad will be glad about that, but I'm still going to have trouble, though. Mrs. Bailey's leaving for a vacation this weekend. I don't know what to do about Tessa." Then I had an idea. "Hey, Rusty, how about your mom? She's home most of the time. Could Tessa go over to your house for a couple of hours?"

He hesitated a long time before answering. "Gee, I don't know, Callie. Mom's always so busy."

His mother bakes breads and cookies from pine nuts, and she makes cactus jellies and candies to sell to a little souvenir and tea shop in Rancho Palms. "Tessa could help her. She's getting to be quite a cook. You wouldn't believe some of the salads she makes."

"I guess you could ask Mom."

Rusty started humming off-key. Sometimes he drives me crazy with it. But now the humming didn't bother me. It gave me a chance to think about Kurt.

For a mile and a half or so we made our way

through stickery brush down a trail I'd been on before. But when we turned off onto what was little more than an animal path, I was totally lost. Rusty's humming cut off abruptly. He stopped and looked around.

We had come to the end of a box canyon. There was nothing but high canyon walls all around us. I could almost imagine that coyotes were peering at us from their dens.

"So where is this great place of yours?"

"The opening is right here somewhere."

"Wonderful. We're lost," I said.

"We're not lost." He was pushing aside spiky mesquite and cats claw. "I found it."

He held aside the bushes with a stick so I could get through easier. But even then the thorns and stickers caught on my clothes and scratched my hands and face.

"I should wear armor when I go hiking with you," I said. "This place better be worth it."

I followed Rusty and Cocoa through an opening in a rock wall and stepped into another world. For a minute I couldn't say anything at all. "Ooh," I whispered. "It's fantastic."

We were in a glade with trees, ferns, and trailing vines. The ground was soft and mossy with tiny white flowers everywhere. Sun filtered through the leaves and glimmered on a large pool. This place was almost as beautiful as some of my fantasy lands.

Rusty was grinning. "I knew you'd like it. I found some Indian pottery. But I'll bet nobody else has been here in ages. Come on."

To get to the pool we had to cross a marshy area. As we waded through mud and ooze, my tennis shoes squished with every step. Birds and frogs protested loudly.

"See all this buckwheat?" Rusty asked.

I think he knows every plant that grows in California.

"I'll bet this is where the Indians came to grind buckwheat and get water before they crossed the desert."

I knew how much it meant to him to find this place, and I was really touched that he'd want to share it with me. "It's great, Rusty, just great. Thanks."

I followed him to a fallen log near the pool. We both got down on our knees to drink the cool spring water. I drank so much I practically sloshed.

Rusty opened his pack and handed me a nut bread and cream cheese sandwich and an orange.

"I'll bet this'll be an important archeological dig," Rusty said.

I'll bet Kurt would like this place, I thought.

"There might even be plants and animals that only exist here," Rusty added, "like in those movies about dinosaurs."

Maybe Mom would invite Kurt to a barbecue some Sunday and I could bring him here.

Rusty didn't say anything for a long time. But every so often I would catch him looking at me, and he'd quickly look away. Finally he blurted, "Callie, Mom's taking me to Disneyland for my birthday. She said I could invite a friend. Do you want to go?"

The last thing I wanted to do was go someplace with his mom tagging along. Pam would never let me live it down. "Gee, I don't know if I'll have to babysit. Can I let you know later?" Maybe by then I could think of a way to say no without hurting his feelings.

"Sure."

Cocoa paddled around for a bit then settled down on the bank to watch a frog sitting on a lily pad. They had a conversation. "Croak." "Growl." "Rib-bett." "Grrrrr."

I was ready to leave, but I could tell Rusty still had something on his mind. Maybe I'd really hurt his feelings because I hadn't jumped at the chance to go with him to Disneyland. Why should I worry about his mom going along? It wasn't a real date.

Anyway, how else would we get there, for Pete's sake? "Russ, I'll probably be able to go on your birthday. That's a Saturday, isn't it?"

"Uh huh. I sure hope you can make it."

"I think I can unless we go down to San Diego. Did Kurt tell you he invited me out on his yacht? How come you don't ever go? Imagine being on a yacht?"

"Callie, I don't know how to bring this up. Promise you won't get mad?"

"I won't get mad."

He took a deep sigh. "It's just that I don't want you to get hurt."

"What are you talking about?" I asked, but my mind was on Kurt.

"He's too old for you," Rusty mumbled.

I jerked my head up to stare at him. "Are you talking about Kurt?"

"Yes," he said with a groan. "I knew you'd be mad. Just forget it. It's none of my business."

"No, it's not any of your business," I said angrily. "Did he say something to you about me yesterday?"

"No, but I saw the way you looked at him the other day. And Pam and Lynn say he's all you talk about. They said you're going to go out on his yacht and everything."

"I'll never tell Lynn anything again in my

entire life. What do you guys do, spend all your time talking about me?"

"No," he said miserably. "Please, Callie, forget I said anything. Here, have a cookie. It's made of pine nuts."

"I don't want any more to eat. I just lost my appetite."

Rusty put all our wrappers into his backpack and left the cookies for the rabbits.

The day was spoiled for both of us. On the way home we hardly spoke a word. Rusty didn't even hum. When we got to my place, he apologized again.

I just nodded.

I could feel his eyes on me as I went inside. He's got sadder brown eyes than his darned dog. I turned to wave and to say thanks for sharing his special place with me.

But he was gone.

Nine

OVER the weekend I read some of my library books, especially the ones on lifesaving. I intended to impress Kurt with my knowledge.

I was still burned over Lynn, Rusty, and Pam discussing me behind my back. I switched on the telephone answering machine so I wouldn't have to talk to them.

On Monday, I rushed around getting all my chores done. Mrs. Long agreed to watch Tessa for three hours on the days of my class. Of course, Tessa was furious. "I wish we had a portable computer," she yelled.

I nearly went nuts before I finally got to the pool and signed up. There were only eight other kids taking the course. I was glad, because Kurt would have more time to give us special attention.

First, Kurt gave us a little talk about the

American Red Cross. "Most of you know about the great work the Red Cross does in times of disaster. I hope none of you ever need their help, but you can prepare yourself for many emergencies. The Red Cross gives all kinds of courses—water safety, swimming, and lifesaving. There are classes on first aid, instructor aides, boating safety, kayaking, sailing, home nursing, and even classes on good grooming and babysitting."

All the kids groaned at that, me the loudest.

"And there's a course called Facts for Life."

Another groan.

He grinned at everyone. "Not facts *of* life. It's about banking, personal budgeting, and job hunting. You can get a complete list of classes at the office."

He passed out some pamphlets on Basic Rescue and Water Safety. "The actual class time takes about six hours. But I like to make sure that everybody understands everything completely. So you can plan on about two weeks.

"Now, before you take your swimming tests, I'll tell you what equipment you'll need. Get a mask made of soft, flexible rubber with an untinted, shatterproof safety glass facepiece. You'll need fins that fit properly so you don't get leg cramps or chafed feet. And you'll need a good snorkel. Don't bring any cheap toys. They can be dangerous. If anyone has a problem getting good equipment, you come and see me. Okay? Any questions?"

One boy held up his hand. "Will I be able to skin-dive in the ocean after this course?"

"No. You should take a regular class for that."

I had been glancing through the booklet and saw a section on floating. I held up my hand. "Will I pass the test if I can't float?"

"Don't worry. You'll know how. Unless of course, you fill your swimsuit with bricks."

Everybody laughed, and I wished I had never admitted I couldn't float.

Next, we took our swimming tests. We had to do five swimming strokes. All the kids passed.

Before we left for the day, Kurt showed us a chart with our names. "You'll be able to see how you're doing on all aspects of the course. If you score low on one thing, you can put in a little extra work on your own. You all did just great today. See you Wednesday."

The first lesson was over much too fast. I wanted to talk to him, but I didn't dare. I'd miss my bus.

When I got home, Tessa said Lynn had called. But by the time I got through helping clean up the kitchen I was beat. I forgot to call her back.

The next day, Tuesday, was Mom's day off. I figured I wouldn't be stuck with Tessa.

I waited until Mom had her cup of coffee and was reading the paper, then asked, "Can I go to the pool today, Mom?"

"You're already going three times a week."

"But that's class. I don't get to do any swimming. Can't I have some fun just one day a week?"

"Oh, all right. Help me clean house this morning, and you can go right after lunch."

I called Lynn to see if she wanted to go, but nobody was home.

*   *   *   *   *

The trip to the pool was a washout. It was Kurt's day off.

Wednesday finally came. This time Kurt talked about how drowning was the second cause of accidental death in America for people from four to forty-four. He told us there were three basic rules for personal safety in emergencies—don't panic, take time to think, and save your strength.

"I know some of you just finished Kim Albright's course on Basic Water Safety, but

I'd like to review a few things for the rest of you.

"Diving into unknown water is dangerous. Stay out of the water during lightning storms. Never swim alone or when you're overheated."

My mind drifted off. I was watching Kurt. I loved the way his lips moved when he talked and how his eyes seemed to spark when he smiled. I brought myself up short. Okay, Callie, you're here to learn. Do you want him to think you're a bubblehead?

"There are many ways to help a drowning person without actually rescuing them in the water," Kurt was saying. "Reaching assists are the safest methods for both the victim and rescuer. Reach with an arm, a leg, a pole, a towel, a branch, a paddle. Or you can throw a ring buoy if you're at a pool. If you're on a picnic or outing, you can use a picnic chest, a large thermos bottle, even a spare tire."

He started to talk about cramps, and my face turned red. For a minute I thought he meant period cramps. But of course he was talking about cramps from overexertion and from getting too tired. "Just remember this, kids. There isn't much danger unless you panic."

Then he went into getting caught in riptides and weeds. I didn't figure I'd run into too many of them in the pool. But it would be good to know when I went out on Kurt's yacht.

He reviewed mouth-to-mouth resuscitation, using a dummy. Oh, that lucky dummy, I thought.

When we were through for the day, I went over to Kurt. "You're a wonderful teacher," I said. "I really learned a lot today."

"Good. I think everybody should know how to swim and how to deal with emergencies."

"Well, I just wanted you to know, I'm glad I signed up for your course."

"The next session will be more fun. You'll get to do more things in the water."

I glanced at the clock. "If I miss my bus I'll have to walk home."

I was sort of hinting about a ride in his car, but he just said, "You'd better hurry. I don't want you to get in trouble with your dad."

He gave me a little pat on the shoulder, and my legs turned to noodles. I stood watching him cleaning up around the pool for so long I nearly did miss my bus.

That evening I called Lynn. She was just leaving to have dinner with Pam and her mother.

"I tried to get you over the weekend," she said. "But you didn't call back. Do you want to go skating tomorrow?"

"I can't. I made a deal to babysit Tessa until it's time to go to the pool."

"It seems like you never have time for anything, anymore."

"Well, it's not my fault I have a dumb little sister."

"It's not just her. All you ever talk about is that lifeguard and the pool and swimming," she said.

I clenched my teeth together so I wouldn't say anything mean. "You used to be interested in the things I liked."

"I am, but I'm tired of hearing about 'dear wonderful Kurt.'"

"I'm sorry I bore you," I said, and hung up. Then I felt awful.

Lynn just doesn't understand how I feel about Kurt . . .

* * * * *

The next few sessions were really fun. We learned underwater swimming, diving, towing an unconscious person, and how to use the mask and fins. I had borrowed Rusty's mask and snorkel. But I'd had to buy my own fins, because his feet are bigger than mine.

The first day I wore the mask and fins I felt like the swamp monster galumping around.

One guy tried to do a tap dance until Kurt bawled him out.

"Okay, kids, settle down. Remember I said you should always swim with a buddy? It's the same with diving. So we're going to pair up."

I had already noticed we were an uneven number. I managed to be looking for my snorkel under the bench while he divided the kids into pairs. I figured if I didn't have a buddy, Kurt would have to help me.

So much for great plans. Kim came in to help. Guess who my buddy was?

I didn't even get personal attention with floating. I had always tried to float face up, but Kurt taught us survival floating, a "drown-proofing" technique. Kurt said with this method a person can stay afloat for hours.

Crumb! I was able to do it easily.

That Wednesday after class I found Lynn waiting for me out front. "Hey," I said, "Are you going to catch the bus?"

"Yeah. I just got through with gymnastics."

I was really glad to see her. I'd felt awful about hanging up on her. "That's great. I have a zillion things to tell you."

"Callie? Oh, Callie, wait up."

I turned to see Kurt coming out of the building. He was holding up a snorkel. He hurried over to us. "I'm glad I caught you before you got away. I think this is yours. It has Rusty's name on it."

"Thanks. It's mine, all right." I felt stupid. "I don't know how I managed to forget it," I said.

He was smiling at Lynn. "I met you the other day, didn't I? You're a friend of Rusty's, too."

She just stood there grinning and nodding yes.

"I tried to talk Lynn into signing up for your class."

"I have gymnastics on Wednesday," Lynn said.

"She's a great gymnast. You should see her on the balance beam."

"I really admire gymnasts," he said. Then he turned to me. "Callie, we'll be through with this class on Friday. I hope you've signed up for Advanced Lifesaving."

"I thought you told me you had to be fifteen for that," Lynn said.

Kurt looked at me, and I turned a thousand shades of red. "You mean you aren't fifteen?"

I glared at Lynn. Now, she'd ruined everything. I couldn't look him in the eye. "No," I mumbled.

Kurt laughed. I knew he was laughing at me, a dumb kid trying to be older.

"I'm going to miss the bus," I said and rushed off.

Lynn caught up with me at the bus stop. "Callie, I'm sorry. I didn't know you'd lied to him about your age."

"I didn't lie! But I don't see why you had to bring it up. You made me look like a fool."

"Don't be silly. Why should he care one way or the other?"

"I care! Now, he's going to think I'm a stupid little kid. Now, he'll never want me to go on his yacht."

"I said I was sorry. It's not the end of the world, you know."

"I don't want to talk about it. You've spoiled everything for me."

I was glad to see the bus pull up. I dropped my money in the coin box and hurried to the middle of the bus. I found a seat and put my bag beside me so Lynn couldn't sit there.

She stopped, and I could feel her eyes on me. But I stared out the window. After a moment, she took a seat in the back. When we got to Desert Willow, I got off the bus before our regular stop and walked the rest of the way home. Instead of going in the house right away, I went to my special place to think.

He must think I'm a real jerk. Over and over I could hear him laugh and say, You mean you're not fifteen? How could Lynn have done that to me? Pam, yes, but not Lynn. Maybe I didn't know her as well as I thought I did.

The wind had come up and it was getting chilly now. I glanced at my watch. I was going to catch it for sure. I grabbed my stuff and ran home.

I tried to sneak in the back way, but Mom and Tess were fixing dinner. Mom started to bawl me out, but when she looked at me, she motioned for Tessa to leave the room.

"What's wrong, Callie? You look as if you've lost your last friend."

I just did, I thought.

"Want to talk about what's bothering you?"

"No."

"You're always complaining that I never talk to you," she said.

"I don't want to talk now. Okay?"

"All right. You know where to find me."

That night in bed, I lay awake a long time thinking about Lynn and all the fun we'd had together. And I thought about Kurt, going over and over the times I'd spent with him. I didn't really want to face him, but I had to go back to finish the class or Dad would have a fit.

Sometime near dawn a coyote yapped and then howled mournfully. I think he must have felt just like me . . . alone.

Ten

THE next day when I got to the pool, Kurt was talking to Kim. He saw me come in and motioned me over to the lifeguard chair. "Callie, I was just talking to Kim about you. She teaches an instructor aide course in water safety. Since you meet all the requirements, we thought you might be interested in taking it."

I knew he was referring to my age. I avoided looking at him. "I . . . uh . . . don't know if I could get here. I have to take care of my sister, and she doesn't like to swim."

"That's no problem," Kim said. "Bring her along. There are lots of things for her to do. There's supervised volleyball, softball, story hour at the library, all kinds of things."

"I don't know." I leaned against the tall chair. "I have responsibilities at home."

"It's only an eighteen hour course. It's so

worthwhile, I'm sure your parents would help you find the time," she said.

"We really need you," Kurt added. "Kim and I have to help each other out because we don't have any instructor aides."

The rest of the kids in the class were coming in now, yelling and laughing.

"I hope you'll sign up," Kim said. "It will start next Tuesday." Then she looked up at Kurt. "I'll see you later," she said softly, and took off across the deck to the exit.

"Well," Kurt said to me, "what about it? I'd sure like to have you as my aide. We'd be a great team."

"I don't know. I might even flunk Basic Rescue."

"Not a chance," Kurt said. "You're one of the best in my class."

"I'll think about it." I started to go to put my bag and towel on a bench.

"Callie, wait a minute," Kurt said. "I want to talk to you."

I kept my back to him and stared at my feet.

"Look, I know you were embarrassed because I found out you weren't old enough for the class. But, please don't be. Age isn't important between friends. I'd like you if you were eight or eighty."

I turned and looked up at him. "Really?"

"Really," Kurt said. He smiled.

There went the kangaroos again. "Oh . . . uh . . . me, too . . . I mean . . ."

"I know what you mean." He gave me a warm smile. He leaned over and was looking at my face. "Hey, young lady, you're not wearing a waterproof sunscreen, are you?"

I could only shake my head.

He touched the tip of my nose. "You're going to burn that cute little nose of yours."

It's a wonder I didn't melt down to a little puddle at his feet.

"Last night I decided to have a pool party at my house. It will be tomorrow, in the morning before it gets too hot, about ten. I know it's short notice, but I'd like you to come as my special guest."

I just stood there with my mouth opening and closing, but no words would come out. Finally, I swallowed hard and managed, "Thank you."

"I live at 2233 West Palm Drive," he said. "Hope I'll see you there." He looked at the clock. "It's time for class," he said. "Let's get to work."

Special guest. Special guest. I was special, special, special . . .

* * * * *

On the last day we learned about recovery of a submerged victim. But mostly we reviewed what we'd learned the last two weeks. I couldn't believe how fast the time had gone by. I had really worked hard and my chart showed it. Kurt had graded us from one to ten, and all my scores were either nines or tens.

We finished a little early and were all sitting on the steps of the pool.

"I want to compliment all of you on doing a great job. You've been one of the best classes I've ever taught. I hope all of you who are fifteen and older will sign up for Advanced Lifesaving."

I stared at the cement steps so I wouldn't catch his eyes.

"I'll be starting that class next week."

"What kind of stuff will we learn in it?" one kid asked.

"Well, since we have some time left, why don't I give you a demonstration. Callie, how about being the victim?"

"Do I have to be unconscious?" I asked, trying to make a joke to cover how I felt. "I hate being pulled by the hair."

"We'll try the cross chest carry."

We waded into deeper water, and Kurt pulled me close to his chest. My head rested on his shoulders and chest, and I was practically riding on his hip. I could feel his arm muscles, and I wondered if he could feel my heart pounding in my chest. My head felt as if it were going to burst, and I realized I was holding my breath.

"Relax, Callie," he said softly.

He swam the width of the pool with me, then said, "Okay, now you try it on me."

I was so nervous at the idea, I nearly drowned both of us.

"Kids, remember what I told you about getting panicky? Callie is a good example. Now, take a deep breath, and start over," he told me.

This time I did it perfectly. Well, almost. He's probably going to have a bunch of bruises on his legs from where I kicked him.

He let us go, then. "See you all Monday for your tests."

I smiled to myself. Not me. I'd be seeing him tomorrow. In a daze of happiness I gathered up my things. I changed into my clothes and headed for the bus. The ride home seemed to take only a minute.

Rusty was waiting at the bus stop.

"Hi," I said. "Where are you going so late?"

"Nowhere. I was waiting for you."

"I have to pick up a pizza for dinner tonight," I told him.

"I won't keep you long."

We hadn't really talked for nearly two weeks. I had avoided him ever since he took me down the canyon. I realized I hadn't even helped him get Tornado ready for the parade. "Boy, have I ever been busy," I said, which wasn't much of an excuse.

"You never did tell me whether you're going to Disneyland tomorrow."

"Tomorrow? Oh, my gosh, tomorrow is your birthday, isn't it?"

"Kurt's invited me to a pool party, so Mom will take me there for a little while before we head to Disneyland. Can you go?"

"Oh, Rusty, I forgot all about it. I wish you had reminded me."

"I tried to, but you don't answer your phone calls, and you're always so busy at the pool. That's why I waited for you here."

"Rusty, I'm sorry, but I already have a date for Kurt's pool party. He invited me as his special guest. I couldn't very well just take off in the middle of his party."

"Oh . . . sure . . ." I could tell Rusty was stunned. "I guess not. Well, I'll see you there."

I wanted to kick myself for telling him about the date. I mean, it wasn't exactly a real date. When was I going to learn to keep my mouth shut?

I watched him take off at a run. I felt bad about hurting his feelings, but I hadn't said I'd go with him. He should have reminded me sooner, for Pete's sake.

I felt both crummy and excited all at once. I hurried across the highway to Andy's pizza parlor.

I ordered the large family-size with everything on it. "Take a seat, Callie," Andy said. "It'll be a few minutes."

I started to head for the waiting area.

"Callie?"

I recognized Pam's voice. I turned to see Lynn and Pam at one of the little tables.

"Hi," I said coldly.

Pam motioned to me.

Reluctantly, I went over to their table. "I just have a minute before my pizza's ready."

Lynn didn't look at me.

"We saw Rusty talking to you," Pam said. "Did he ask you to go to Disneyland with him?"

"Yes, but I already have a date with Kurt."

I'd wanted to brag to them about it, but as soon as the words were out of my mouth I knew it was a mistake. Pam glommed onto it like a hungry coyote.

"You have a date with Kurt Saunders? The lifeguard?" Pam shot me a skeptical look. "I don't believe it. Come off it, Callie. Why would an older guy like him even look at you?"

"Because . . . just because."

"Some dumb answer," Pam said.

"For your information, Kurt says the difference in our ages doesn't matter to him at all."

"You're out of your gourd if you think he likes you."

"If he didn't like me why would he invite me out on his yacht? Why would he want me to take the instructor aide course and work with him?"

"He's only nice to you because of Rusty."

"That's a lie!"

"Forget it," Lynn said. "It's her business if she . . ." Lynn stopped. But I knew she had intended to say—if she wants to make a fool of herself.

Trying to pretend I didn't care what they thought, I shrugged. "See you two around."

* * * * *

At dinner I decided not to mention the pool party yet, but only bring up the course. "Mom? Dad? Is it okay if I sign up to be an instructor aide? The lifeguard said I was one of the best in his class and wants me to work with him. Isn't that a great opportunity?"

"Now, I'll never get to work on the computer," Tessa whined.

"How much time is it going to take?" Mom wanted to know.

"It's an eighteen hour course, and it starts next week."

"I don't think so, Callie," Dad said. "It's not fair to Tessa or to your mother."

"But I have that all figured out. I'll stay home until it's time to leave so Tessa can work on the computer. I'll fix most of the meal before I leave. It means a lot to me."

"She just wants to be near . . ." Tessa began.

I gave her a don't-you-dare-mention-Kurt look and she finished with, "near the water."

"You're always getting after me to do something worthwhile, and this is plenty worthwhile."

Mom and Dad looked at each other and nodded. "I suppose it's all right," Dad said. "But you'd better see that dinner's ready before you leave. Your mother is too tired by the time she gets home."

"And no griping about staying with Tessa," Mom put in.

"Yeah," Tessa said. "And tell her she can't boss me around all the time."

I ignored her and kissed Mom and Dad. "I promise. Thanks."

After dinner I brought up the party. "I've been invited to a party tomorrow morning in Rancho Palms."

"Who's giving it?" Mom asked.

I had never told them about Kurt working at the paper. "Dad, do you remember a Kurt Saunders who was a paperboy for you five or six years ago?"

He shook his head. "I've had dozens and dozens of paperboys in that time."

"Well, he remembers you. Says you were a wonderful boss." I didn't bring up the broken screen doors. "He's from a very wealthy family, and he's my instructor. Can I go?"

"We don't know the Saunders," Mom said.

"Rusty will be there," I told them. "Kurt's a friend of Rusty's."

"Well, I suppose it's all right, if you don't stay too late," Mom agreed.

"Thanks. I won't. Dad can you take me? It starts at ten."

"I guess so, but don't make a habit of this."

"I won't. I promise." I gave them each a hug. "You're the greatest Mom and Dad in the world," I said.

"Oh, brother," Tessa said. "She gets everything she asks for, and I never do."

"You'll get your turn," Mom said.

I almost felt sorry for Tessa. Growing up took such a long time.

* * * * *

Early the next morning I was trying to decide how to fix my hair. Tessa was watching me from her bed. "I think I'll get a haircut," I said.

"Why? You look okay to me."

Surprised at getting a compliment from her instead of a nasty remark, I told her about Kurt. "Oh, Tessa, guess what? Do you remember Kurt, the lifeguard who brought us home?"

"I remember. He's the one you're in love with."

I ignored that remark. "Anyway, he asked me to be his special guest at his party. Don't tell Mom and Dad I have a date. You know them. They'd think I was too young."

"Sure, Callie. Tessa looked pleased. You've never told me anything important before. You never let me in the room when you and Lynn are talking about things."

"Well, we aren't talking about anything important now." I was still looking at my hair. "I think I'll get it cut. I want it just like Kim's.

She's the other lifeguard. She wears her hair short with bangs. Whenever she tosses her head all the hairs fall right back in place."

"I kinda like your hair the way it is," Tessa said.

"It's horrible. I can't do anything with it."

* * * * *

I managed to get an appointment. I took some of my babysitting money and hurried down to the little shop next to the pizza parlor. But when it was too late, I knew I'd made a terrible mistake.

I ran home and stared at myself in the mirror. I wanted to cry. My hair didn't look a bit like Kim's. The hairdresser had tried to talk me out of the cut. She said my hair was too baby-fine to look good that way, but I had insisted.

It looked awful.

Tessa came in to make her bed. "Oh, wow! Did you get it cut with a lawn mower?"

"Don't you dare laugh."

Tessa stared at me solemnly. I couldn't even see her lips twitch. "You look kinda like a scared cotton ball."

"Thanks. I really needed that."

"Ah, it doesn't look that bad." Then her

face began to crumple into a broad grin. She put her hands over her mouth and hooted with laughter.

"Stop it!"

"You look like you stuck your finger in an electric socket." She touched a piece of hair that stuck out.

"Get your dirty little paws off my hair."

"Oh yeah!"

"Can't you ever say anything except, oh yeah? It's positively juvenile."

"And you're positively a creep, and I hope you have a crummy time at your dumb old party."

"Well, you'll never even get invited to one!"

She got the last word, though.

"Daddy got called in to work. He said you'd have to ask a friend or take the bus. He said, no hitchhiking."

"He knows I never hitchhike."

Wasn't anything going to go right? First it was my hair, now this.

"Why don't you ask Rusty?" Tessa suggested. "His mom's taking him."

"I know, but I already turned him down. I told you, I have a date with Kurt."

"Rusty's a lot nicer. He's taking me riding."

Would Rusty take Tessa to his special place? I wondered. A twinge of disappointment ran through me.

It was too late to do anything about my hair, so I stuck on my hat and got dressed in white shorts, a new blue top, and white sandals. I had to run all the way to the bus stop to catch the nine-thirty.

My timing wasn't any better when I got to the Saunders' house. I got off the bus just as Rusty and his mom arrived. And to make it worse, Pam and Lynn were with him.

Rusty didn't even look at me.

"You came on the bus?" Pam said. "Some date."

"I didn't want him to come all the way to Desert Willow," I said quickly.

We all walked to the door together, but no one said anything.

The Saunders' house wasn't anything like my fantasy. It was nice, but not much bigger than Lynn's.

As Rusty rang the bell, Pam whispered, "You'd think with all their money, they'd do better than this."

"Some people don't put on a big show of their wealth," I said, but I was a bit disappointed.

Instead of a butler as I'd imagined, a woman a little older than Mom answered the door. She was wearing a tennis outfit, and her hair was all windblown. She was an ordinary, everyday mother.

"Hello Rusty. Happy Birthday."

"Thanks, Mrs. Saunders. "I'd like you to meet my friends, Lynn Adams and Pam Jennings."

He very pointedly avoided looking at me.

Mrs. Saunders turned to me. "And your name, dear?"

"I'm Callie Anderson, Kurt's friend."

"Please come in. The others are all out in back by the pool."

"Lynn, Pam, and I won't be swimming," Rusty said. "My mom will be back in a while to take us to Disneyland, but I promised Kurt I'd stop by."

As we followed her, Pam whispered, "Why didn't Kurt come to the door to greet you. His mother didn't even know your name."

We came out through a sliding glass door to the patio and pool area. Some older kids were in a group by themselves. Everyone was wearing swimsuits. "Darn," I said aloud. "I forgot my suit."

Mrs. Saunders gave me a warm smile that reminded me of Kurt. "We always keep extra swimsuits in the bathhouse." She pointed to a little building near the pool. "I'm sure you can find a suit to fit."

"Thanks," I said, returning her smile.

Pam turned to me. She was smirking. "So you have a date with Kurt, do you? Well, if you're his date, what's he doing over there." She pointed to the group of older kids. "There's your date."

Kurt was standing next to Kim. His arm was around her waist, and she was laughing up at him. He bent and kissed her.

I could feel Rusty's and Lynn's eyes on me. My face burned. My insides shriveled into a hard knot. For a moment I couldn't think, couldn't feel, couldn't move.

Oh, I was really special, all right. What a fool, what a dumb, blind fool. Trying to save face, I said brightly, "I think I'll change into a suit and get some tan." I headed quickly to the bathhouse. I sat there on a bench for a few minutes, dry-eyed, empty.

I heard Kurt say, "Hi, Russ, glad you could make it." He didn't even ask about me.

I knew I couldn't face anybody so I slipped quietly into the house. I was almost out the door when Kurt's mother called to me. "You're not leaving so soon, are you?"

"I'm not feeling too great. Would you thank Kurt for inviting me?"

"Of course. Do you want me to drive you home?"

"No, that's okay. I'll just catch the bus."

I thanked her again and went out to the bus stop. I glanced at my watch. The next bus wouldn't go to Desert Willow for nearly an hour. I decided to walk home by the horse trail.

At least with something to do and a definite plan, I didn't feel quite so bad. I headed for the nearest store and bought juice in cartons. It was hot out, and I knew I'd get plenty thirsty.

About a mile from Kurt's house, I picked up the trail. It was cooler than the highway and the dirt path was easier on my feet. As I trudged up the steadily climbing trail, I tried to shove all the embarrassment and pain to the back of my mind. But Kurt's and Kim's faces kept flashing in front of my eyes. And Pam's voice rang in my ears. *If you're his date, what's he doing? What's he doing? What's he doing . . .*

I was never going to be able to face anyone again.

The first couple of miles weren't too hard. I'm used to hiking, but my sandals kept filling with sand and dirt, and cholla cactus scratched my bare legs. It was so hot. The sun was right overhead. Salty sweat dripped down my face and neck. My shirt was plastered against my back. I stopped only once to drink the last of my juice, but it didn't quench my thirst.

The last mile was almost straight up hill. My legs felt so heavy I could hardly move them. My feet were blistered. Rusty would have scolded me, but I took off my sandals.

With my house in sight, I got a boost of energy and almost ran the rest of the way home. But then I changed my mind. I didn't want to have to deal with Tessa, so I headed for the spot where I could be alone and think.

I sat under the willow tree and for the first time since I saw Kurt kissing Kim, I broke down and cried.

Eleven

I don't know how long I sat there crying, when I heard footsteps. I jumped up and started to run.

"Wait up, Callie. I have to talk to you."

It was Lynn. "How did you know where I was?"

"I stopped by your house. Tessa saw me and told me you come up here when you're feeling bad."

Tessa had never let on that she knew about this place. I turned away from Lynn and leaned against the trunk of the willow. "I thought you and Pam were going to Disneyland with Rusty?"

"They're waiting for me in front of your house. We were worried about you. So we drove back to see if you were okay."

"Of course I'm okay. I didn't mean for anybody to worry about me."

"Callie? Turn around and look at me. I know how you must have felt when you saw Kurt kissing another girl."

"Nobody knows . . ." I turned around, and she saw my tear-stained face.

"Oh, Callie."

We rushed toward each other and hugged.

"I'm glad you're not mad at me any more," Lynn said. "I've been miserable."

"Me, too. You're my best friend. Only best friends can afford to get mad at each other." I wiped my eyes and grinned. "I heard that on our soap opera."

"I don't blame you for being mad at me," Lynn said. " I'm really sorry about telling Kurt your real age."

"I guess I felt kind of left out because you've been spending so much time with Pam."

"My mom wanted me to because of the divorce. Pam feels awful about her folks splitting up." Then Lynn looked sheepish. "And I felt jealous of Kurt. You never talked about anything else."

"I'm sorry I spoiled the party for you," I said.

"Oh, it wasn't much fun, anyway. Most of the kids were older. Callie, what about your test? Don't you take it Monday?"

"I'm never going back to the pool, not as long as he's a lifeguard there. I never want to see him again."

We were both quiet for a moment, then I said, "You'd better get going and not keep them waiting any longer."

"Why don't you come, too?"

"I couldn't face Rusty. He must really hate me."

"He was plenty burned, all right."

"I should have listened to you when you said Kurt flirted with all the girls. I made such a fool of myself, telling everybody I had a date. Oh, Lynn, I'll never love anybody again."

*　*　*　*　*

The next day while Tessa was outside talking to one of her friends, I went into the office to check on the telephone answering machine. I sat at the desk to listen, whirling around on the typewriter chair. There were no messages on the machine, but I noticed Tessa had left the computer on. I was surprised that she hadn't taken out the diskettes and turned it off. Whatever she was working on was still showing on the screen.

I read the file name at the bottom of the screen. B:diary7.MSS. The crazy kid was actually keeping a diary in the computer. Nobody but my sister would do that.

I had no intention of reading the green words on the screen, but my name caught my eye, and I had to read what the little twerp had said about me.

Oh, diary, I wish I was 13. I wish I was more like Callie. She can do practically anything. She's so pretty. I shouldn't have laughed at her haircut. She already felt bad about it.

But, diary, nobody ever, ever cares how I feel. I guess they don't think kids have feelings, and if I didn't have you to talk to I'd want to run away.

Oh, I can hardly wait to be old enough for a boy like Rusty to ask me to a real party. He's WONDERFUL. He never treats me like a little kid. I know he likes Callie a whole lot, but he'll always be my secret, best-ever person.

Dear diary, I know I've said some mean things about Callie, but I never really meant it. I wish I could tell her I'm glad she's my big sis

She had stopped in the middle of the word. I swallowed the huge lump in my throat. I'd forgotten how it felt to be ten. And Tessa didn't know yet that even when she got to be my age, she'd still be wondering why she was too young.

I had to admit though, I was acting more

like a little kid than Tessa was. She knew that Rusty could only be a good friend to her. Hadn't Kurt said he'd like me if I were eight or eighty? He'd meant, like me as a friend. I'd tried to make it more than that.

I left the office and quietly closed the door behind me. I went out to the kitchen. I looked at her for a minute. She wasn't such a bad kid, after all. "Tessa," I said, "I have to go up to Rusty's for a little while."

I fairly flew up the hill to Rusty's house. He was in the corral with his horses. The smell seemed even stronger than ever. He looked up and saw me, then turned back to his work.

"Rusty?" I said softly.

"Yes," he said, still with his back to me.

"Got a minute?"

"Not really. I have work to do before it gets dark."

"It won't take long."

"Are you feeling okay now? They said you went home sick."

"I wasn't sick. I just couldn't face anybody, especially you."

He pulled off his work gloves and leaned against the fence. "So?"

"So, I came to apologize for acting like a little kid and for treating my friends as if they had no feelings."

I stopped, but I could see he wasn't going to help me get through this. "I came to ask you a big favor, but I sure wouldn't blame you if you said no. As Pam said, I've been a pain."

He nodded emphatically.

"You could argue with me a little," I said, trying to smile. "Anyway, I wanted to ask you this. I'll do anything, even bag manure . . ." I made a face. ". . . if you'd just be my friend again." My voice trailed off.

He picked up his gloves and the shovel and held them out. "So, get busy. We have to have all this bagged by noon."

"If you still want me to, I can help you get Tornado ready for the parade . . . starting Tuesday, after my test."

Rusty grinned. "Glad you're back, Callie." He gave me a little punch on the arm, and would you believe it, the kangaroos began playing hopscotch in my stomach.

Maybe all sun gods don't ride white stallions past the moon and the sun. Maybe, just maybe, one rides a brown and white pinto pony through canyons and deserts.